Dead and Living

Dead and Living

A NOVEL

by Jane Bow

A MIDNIGHT ORIGINAL

The Mercury Press

While the events in the court case recounted in this book are faithful to those in the actual
trial, all characters described herein, and the stories of their lives, are strictly fictitious.

ACKNOWLEDGEMENTS

The author wishes to extend her appreciation to Janet Lunn for her many hours of
invaluable guidance, and to all those involved in the actual court case who provided help
and encouragement. Most especially she thanks Grant, Christopher and Sarah Collins,
Malcolm and Betty Bow, Michael Bow and Kelly Anderson, and Neil and Leslie Bow for
their love and support.

The publisher gratefully acknowledges the financial assistance of the Canada Council and
the Ontario Arts Council, as well as that of the Government of Ontario
through the Ontario Publishing Centre.

Cover design: Gordon Robertson
Cover photograph: Doug Forster

Composition in Goudy Old Style by TASK.
Printed and bound in Canada by Metropole Litho.

CANADIAN CATALOGUING IN PUBLICATION:
Bow, Jane
Dead and Living
ISBN 0-920544-96-7
I. Title.
PS8553.O8D4 1993   C813'.54   C93-094765-7
PR9199.3.B6D4 1993

Canadian Sales Representation by the Literary Press Group.

The Mercury Press is distributed in Canada by General Publishing,
and in the United States by Inland Book Company (selected titles).

The Mercury Press
137 Birmingham Street
Stratford, Ontario
Canada N5A 2T1

For Grant, with love

&

In memory of Paul

✿ BEFORE ✿

The car is fishtailing. Headlights strafe the frozen bush like the crazed eyes of some other-world Goliath. Rodger grips the back of the seat in front of him, peers out the window, through the driving snow into darkness. There's something out there, something moving. A man?

Impossible. It's forty below in this godforsaken place.

The car swerves again. And there it is, clear now: it is a man, no, several men, coming towards the speeding car. Muffled in ragged coats against the cold, they move in slow motion, coming closer, slowly closer, in spite of the car's speed. Their faces look yellow in the headlights, lifeless, their mouths are hollow holes opening and closing soundlessly as they point at the snowbank, a ten-foot cliff beside the road. The car stops. Rodger begins to shake. He knows he has to get out, has to hear the snow crunch under his boots as he climbs the snowbank, has to watch as the corpse staggers to its feet in the ditch on the other side, the snow still lying like confetti in its hair, on its eyelashes, the blood dripping from the side of its head while the dead black eyes stare at him and the dead arm slowly rises, its finger pointing...

"No!"

Rodger blinks, finds himself sitting up in his cot. There is the yard lamp outside his cell window. He takes a breath, rubs the bridge of his nose, shivers in the pre-dawn cold. The horror of the dream lingers with him, as always, real as the sweat on his skin. Real as memory.

Except that there is no memory... Is there?

⚚ CHAPTER 1 ☙

The man in the prisoner's box does not look like a murderer. Killers, in my meagre experience, are colourless people in borrowed grey suits, people in whom a once-in-a-lifetime eruption of rage has collided with circumstance, not the sort of people you would glance at twice in the street. This one is different, though...

"Oyez, oyez, oyez. All persons having anything to do before my Lord the Queen's Justice of the Supreme Court of Ontario at this the November 1972 sitting of assize and *nisi prius*, oyer and terminer, and general gaol delivery for the District of Thunder Bay draw near and give your attendance and you shall be heard. God save the Queen." The clerk's archaic words have come down to us from the days of knights and heralds' trumpets.

Behind the clerk, up on the bench, Mr. Justice William Harley, wearing the traditional black robe and red cummerbund, waits in this room where burgundy velvet curtains and oak panelling have closed out the rain-soaked November afternoon outside. The faces of the jury, ranged in two rows along the side wall in front of my press table, have a smooth, churchy look. The clerk glances over his bi-focals at the prisoner. They are the only two people left standing.

"Rodger Pearse Brown alias Jones, you stand charged that on or about the thirteenth day of April in the year 1947, you did unlawfully murder one Raymond Boucher, a taxi driver at Geraldton, Ontario, contrary to the Criminal Code of Canada. How do you plead?"

There is silence.

The prisoner looks to be in his mid-fifties. He is wearing a grey suit, a size too large— from the stock of clothing defense lawyer Peter

Cosselli keeps in his office closet— but there is an unusual dignity in the way Brown carries it. Something to do with the set of his shoulders and head, the wavy grey hair, and the way his glance skittered through the courtroom when the bailiff brought him in, his concern on finding the two elderly people sitting by themselves behind a phalanx of police witnesses.

Now he stands gripping the wooden railing that crosses the courtroom from just behind my press table, surrounds his prisoner's box then goes on to separate this, the courtroom arena, from the spectators' pews. The clock on the side wall behind me ticks off one minute, two.

The seven men and five women on the jury, who hold the man's future in their hands, begin to fidget, rearranging their bottoms on the hard wooden chairs. They are ordinary people, many of them in their fifties and sixties— a bricklayer, a teacher, a packer, an accountant, a postal clerk, a homemaker— unsure of themselves in this formal, wood-panelled room, wondering why they of all people were chosen this morning from the panel of randomly selected citizens the sheriff had summoned to the District Courthouse.

"Why did you object to that attractive blond woman with the short hair?" I asked Crown attorney Gerald Foss earlier, during the lunch recess. The woman's address is in my neighbourhood.

"The one in the forest green ski jacket, brown slacks?" Foss snorted, "She's the classiest hooker in town. We've been trying to put her out of business for years."

Because Foss's duty is to put upstanding representatives of the community on the jury, jury selection rules allow him to turn down as many people as he likes. His preference is to choose those who will sympathize with the Crown's point of view.

Defense counsel Peter Cosselli is only allowed to challenge a certain number of the people the Crown has chosen. His job is to weed out people who may be prejudiced against his client's interests. Now the chosen dozen wait, their eyes fixed on the prisoner.

Rodger Pearse Brown stares straight ahead at the portrait of the Queen mounted on the wall beside the flagstand, behind the judge. There is definitely something unusual about the man.

Innocence... or a kind of jaded nobility? Surely not. Naivete then? They say he is a seaman, and that he really does not know whether he committed this murder, that he has come halfway across the country to find out...

Also, he is nervous. I swallow, I can relate to that.

As usual I am alone at the press table. Thunder Bay's radio and television stations cannot afford to cover the court beat, so they lift my words verbatim out of the newspaper, sending a reporter only for the climactic moments.

It means that this strange story is mine. If I can create a clear portrait of this man and what the system he is facing does to him, the Canadian Press wire service will send my writing to media across the country. People from Halifax to Vancouver Island will read my words... If I can do the story right...

But I am only twenty-three, less than two years out of university. It is 1972 and so far I have been too busy living my life to know much about what makes people tick. To date, my training has involved wearing Flower Power jeans, high boots and long hair, marching in peace rallies and smoking cigarettes and other funny-smelling substances to the tunes of the Moody Blues, spending long weekends in bed with John, a fellow journalism graduate turned temporary civil servant, making love and then, over porridge eaten out of the pot in bed, plotting how writing the Truth, "telling it like it is," will end the political corruption of the middle-aged, silver-haired, blue-suited WASPs who hold all the power. Hunter S. Thompson is my hero.

After graduation I landed a job writing bike trail brochures in a sleepy back office of Ottawa's National Capital Commission. Then a Toronto newspaper executive answered the query letter in which I had sent sample clippings and a photograph, and invited me to come to Toronto for lunch.

Brimming with hope, also fantasies of imminent national renown, maybe even overseas correspondencies, I brushed out my hair, put on my best mini-dress...

And then wondered, as we sat sipping sherry at Winston's, why he had brought me to one of Toronto's flossiest restaurants. Surely his daily newspaper did not interview all its neophyte reporters here, among the white linen and crystal, fresh carnations on every table? Was I missing something?

He was a stout man in his forties, with blow-dried hair and a suit... not the kind of man you find behind the editor's desk at a large city's daily newspaper.

"Just what kind of a newspaper executive are you?" I ventured over the omelettes.

He smiled silkily. "Let's just say I am powerful enough, and impressed enough, to want to talk more about your future..." So how would I like to adjourn to his apartment with him?

I blinked. And saw myself, suddenly, through his eyes: my hair carefully done, my long legs encased in off-black stockings, my young, eager, incredibly gullible ego as obvious as my lipstick. I lurched to my feet, bringing the edge of the linen table cloth with me, rattling the coffee cups, and went home to cry into John's lap. He stroked me, and then slowly, deliciously, undressed me.

"What does it matter," he whispered, "As long as we're together, who cares where you work?"

I cared. So when the Thunder Bay newspaper advertised for a reporter, I packed my bags, drove my heaterless Volkswagen away from the east and all the politics of sex. I would see John on weekends when one of us could afford stand-by airfare on the midnight plane.

Thunder Bay has turned out, unexpectedly, to be the ideal crucible in which to learn about the interplay of people with life.

Perched on the northern shore of Lake Superior, three hundred miles east of Winnipeg, Thunder Bay is a recent amalgamation of two old and disparate cities. Fort William, built by the Kaministikwa River under the shelter of Mount McKay to the west, was once a thriving trading post. Beside it, to the east, Port Arthur stood at the western end of the Great Lakes waterway, the prairies' gateway to the Atlantic, where busy stevedores once transferred western grain and other goods, and passengers' luggage from mile-long strings of railway cars to the Great Lakes steamers bound for Montreal, Boston, New York... while out in Lake Superior the legendary Sleeping Giant— an island shaped like the body of a man— lay silent.

The Giant still sleeps. Port Arthur's lakeshore railway station is mostly quiet now, and though the great stone Prince Arthur Hotel up the hill, just past the newspaper building, still whispers the presence of very important personages, it is rarely full.

Thunder Bay's grain elevators still store western grain, freight trains rolling across Canada still use the rail lines that zigzag through the city, and there is a paper mill, but the city's main industry now is tourism for the thousands of Canadians travelling the Trans-Canada Highway and for Americans wanting to ski and catch fish and hunt the moose and bear and wolves that share this huge expanse of muskeg and granite-covered wilderness with far flung railway towns, native communities, and some strange individuals.

For the rest of the year the city is left to itself: a centre from which provincial court judges, Crown attorneys and defense lawyers fly out to set up court in the local movie theatres of the more isolated

13

communities; where judges from the Supreme Court of Ontario arrive twice a year to try the district's serious legal cases in this grey stone courthouse. Already, in less than two years, I have explored medical malpractice— wherein a dubious doctor sewing up a hernia allegedly put a stitch through a man's bladder— and extortion, rape, manslaughter and murder.

A third minute ticks by. Why doesn't the man answer the charge?

Could he be sensing, now when it is too late, that the words he speaks will kick-start a juggernaut of justice which, grinding on relentlessly, might just as easily chew him up and spit him out as give him Truth?

Peter Cosselli turns from the lawyers' long table in front of the prisoner's box. A short, trim man with styled black hair and protruding black eyes, he looks at home in his lawyer's black gown and starched white collar. Now he gestures to his client.

The prisoner clears his throat. "Not guilty," says Rodger Pearse Brown. But the words are barely audible.

"My Lord, ladies and gentlemen of the jury, this is a most extraordinary case." Crown attorney Gerald Foss is a slight man too, but where Cosselli wears made-to-measure navy blue suits on the street, Foss is a civil servant: grey hair growing wispy across the top, grey suit under his robe. He is the People's Representative, logical, methodical, imbued with Right. Where Cosselli's black eyes might flash from humour through compassion to blazing anger, even to cruelty when necessary, Foss's blue eyes remain cold. Because although he would deny it, deep down in the roots of Gerald Foss's Anglo-Germanic self is buried the history-nurtured certainty that he is superior. To him, the truth is obvious, firmly based upon evidence gathered by his police force. Foss is not here to listen, to ponder, to consider. He is here to get a conviction for the People. He and the law should prevail.

The fact that he succeeds half the time at most is, to his mind, a source of frustration due to unkind circumstances or poor police performances or gullible juries. Today, however, the game has barely begun. Foss smiles at the jury.

"We are asking a lot of you, ladies and gentlemen, we are asking you to try a man for a murder that happened twenty-five years ago. 1947: it's a long time ago.

"Remember? The war was just over. We were still busy adjusting to peace. Also this northland of ours was just beginning to open up... It was a different world. Yet today this court must journey back into that world to do justice to a young man of twenty-two who never made it past those distant days because one night when he was driving his taxi cab someone shot him in the head."

The Crown attorney hooks his fingers into the watchpockets of his waistcoat, making his gown flare: he is a black bird about to take flight.

"How can we make such a journey, you might wonder. Well, ladies and gentlemen, in fact it will be quite simple. We must turn back the years, yes, resurrect the scene of a terrible winter night in April, 1947. But we do so not to decide, with only our foggy twenty-five-year-old memories to guide us, whether the accused is guilty. Rather we do it to set the stage for what has transpired much more recently." Foss stands up straight, rocks back onto his heels, raises his voice.

"Because, ladies and gentlemen of the jury, statements made by the accused to police just six months ago fit neatly into that scene. You will see how six months ago this man," he waves an arm at the prisoner's box, "this Rodger Pearse Brown alias Jones, went to the

Royal Canadian Mounted Police in Vancouver of his own free will, right out of the blue..." I am writing quickly. This is all quotable.

The defense does not offer an opening statement.

...So, there is to be no explanation in tomorrow morning's newspaper of who this Rodger Pearse Brown is and why he went to the police. Maybe I better not spend too much time on Foss's opening, then.

Somehow I have to balance the story while still getting the essence of the drama across to the early morning, coffee-sipping shopkeepers, business people, shift workers. I need to probe behind the evidence, find a way to get under the surface of the case, feel its heartbeat, smell the heat that triggered the accused man's actions...

If I can do this, then maybe I can call myself a writer.

∽∾ CHAPTER 2 ∽∾

"William Chestleman!"

The old man's body is a jiggling mountain of flesh as he hurries down the aisle and through the gate in the wooden railing, on his way to the witness stand. His face is round and flat as pie dough and, as he passes my press table and then the jury, I wonder whether he was this fat twenty-five years ago when he drove his snowplough along the road from Geraldton to Hearst.

"The road had been closed, see. We had had a weekend storm." Chestleman's voice tinkles with nervousness.

"Which side of the road were you working on, Mr. Chestleman?" asks Foss.

"The right side, going east. I was pushing back the snowbanks, levelling the surface..."

"I see. Would you describe the road for us, sir?"

"...Beg pardon?" Chestleman squints at the Crown attorney. He is not used to being the centre of anyone's attention.

"Just tell us a bit about the place. Take us back there."

"Oh, well... in them days it were just a dirt road cut through the bush... There's a lot of jackpine out there... and birch... Then of course there's the lake." The old man stops, unsure of what is wanted.

Foss nods, encouraging him. "What lake is that?"

"Lake Kenogamisis, just outside of Geraldton. I'd go by it pret' near every day..." Foss nods again, smiling, and gradually the old man's heavy face relaxes. "It can be real pretty out there this time of year, with the sap running red and yellow and orange in the trees..."

I smile. The court circuit has taken me along the dirt road Chestleman is describing and past his lake in the spring. I have seen the daytime thaws that melt the ice on the lake so that even after a new snowfall there are blue-black cracks running across the white on the lake. Baby blue and rust-brown patches where the ice is thinning make nature's own abstract painting: here today, changed again tomorrow.

"What shape was the road in, Mr. Chestleman?"

"Oh, it was a real mess, yes sir. Just a sea of mud during the warm days in spring. Then at night the ruts would freeze hard as rock. That's why I was out there with the plow. After we cleared the snow from the weekend, while it were still cold like, I was levelling her out. That's when I seen..." He glances nervously at Foss.

"Yes? Go on, Mr. Chestleman."

"Well I was high up, see, in my grader, and I seen a pair of rubber boots behind the snowbank, just the toes like, stickin' up out of the snow."

"Could you have seen them from a car?"

"Oh no, sir. That snowbank were six feet high anyway."

"Go on."

"Well sir, I knew I had to go look. So I jumped down out of my machine and climbed the snowbank..." Even after all the years Chestleman's voice shakes. He mops his face with a large red polka dot handkerchief. The rest of us wait, the courtroom completely silent as we perch, all of us— judge, lawyers, jury, witnesses, spectators— with Chestleman on a snowbank one horrific day twenty-five years ago. The man in the prisoner's box leans forward in his seat.

"...The man's eyes were open, but he was dead. So I ran back to my grader and—"

"Excuse me, Mr. Chestleman, but did you recognize the man?"

"No sir... There was so many people coming and going then."

"How did you know he was dead? Did you touch him, feel for a pulse?"

"Oh no, sir," Chestleman shivers, "I knowed he were dead by his eyes, the way they just stared, dead like, at the sky... Then also he... well he were froze, see... stiff like."

"I see. And did you see anything else?"

"Sir?"

"Was there anything else there, a weapon, a car— ?"

"Objection." Cosselli half rises, looking bored, "Counsel is leading."

"Sustained."

Chestleman looks confused. "I didn't see nothin' else."

"So you ran back to your grader," Foss continues, "Then what did you do?"

"I radioed the boss. Then I stayed there until Joe Frazier— he was the Ontario Provincial Police, God rest his soul— showed up with a photographer and Claude Caron. He owned the taxi cab company."

The dead man was identified as one Raymond Boucher, taxi driver.

"Claude Caron!"

A slight man wearing a toothbrush mustache and a black suit, the lapels of which shine from recent ironing, takes the witness stand. He stands there proudly, surveying the Queen and the wood panelling, the flags behind the judge, and it is clear that he is thrilled by his civic responsibility.

"Just for the record, Monsieur Caron, how old were you twenty-five years ago?"

Caron's smile sags.

"How old?... Well now I am sixty-two, so..." He looks down at his fingers, then at the judge, "Please excuse me, Your Honour, I am not so good with the counting. You see I have no education at all—"

"You don't have to apologize for that, monsieur." Mr. Justice William Harley is in his late fifties, an ex-varsity football player with a reputation for a kind, low-key brand of fairness.

"That's right," Cosselli half rises again, smiling at the witness, "I have spent half my life at school and still I need a pencil when it comes to adding and subtracting."

Foss smiles sardonically.

"If it please the court, we know that only too well."

Rodger Pearse Brown frowns, looks from one lawyer to the other.

I am right then, he is naive. He does not know that in spite of the gracious decor and musty air, in here it is slash and parry, point and counterpoint, no holds barred, every move, every word carefully designed to mould the thinking of the twelve good men and women watching from the jury box.

Cosselli and Foss have been exchanging jabs, matching wits in this courtroom for more than twenty years. The youngest son of one of Thunder bay's immigrant railway workers, Peter Cosselli's intelligence and quick wit soon took him beyond the family's thick accent and frame tenement, first into the study of law, then into practice among some of the finest legal minds in Toronto. Finally, the day he was offered a judgeship in the provincial courts, he sat down in a bar and looked at the future:

He could be a judge, the top of the heap, spend his days listening, sitting in judgement over his fellow man...

No, he did not want that.

He could grow rich then, working day and night behind the mirrored glass of Bay Street's office towers or within the invisible confines of the city's Italian community. No. He drained his glass, left the bar.

There was only one right place for Peter Cosselli and that was in the District of Thunder Bay where he could be at home in the role of the maverick, the last man to stand between an individual and the mighty force of the law.

"Where else can I be free to run a case the way I want, represent who I want, take a brace of pheasants, or a dozen eggs for payment if a case interests me?" he told me once in an interview.

After court, he and Foss repair to a Port Arthur bar where copious quantities of the finest Scotch help them turn the tension of their courtroom adversity into a razor-edged jocularity that neither will recall tomorrow.

I gaze across the courtroom at the prisoner. He is trapped now, his fate in the hands of the swordsmen, and he doesn't even know it.

"Take your time, Monsieur Caron," says Foss.

The witness looks uncertainly from the lawyers to the judge.

"I am... I will be sixty-two next month so I must have been... thirty-seven then?"

"Thank you, monsieur," Foss glances at his notes, "I understand you operated a taxi stand in Geraldton in 1947. Now where exactly was your business located?"

"It was about a block away from the Geraldton Hotel," Caron replies eagerly, "I had a... how you say, a little booth and three cars."

"And when did you come to know the deceased?"

"He came to work for me only about two days before. I give him a job because he knows my cousin Louis in Kapuskasing, and he was very young, twenty-two. Also he was French, from Montreal

I think, but I do not know for sure. There were so many guys around in those days..."

He is right. The old newspapers I have dug out talk about the post-war boom that changed this northern wilderness into a mecca for the thousands of jobless soldiers who had come home from the war. Go north, everyone said. Miners had been scooping gold out of the ground there since the mid-thirties. But by the time the war veterans arrived, a drop in the price of gold had shut down most of the mines. All that was left of the boom were the towering mine-heads rusting in the bush. So the veterans went instead to the new lumber camps springing up...

"It was such a crazy time," Caron says, "All week the town was quiet, respectable, then every Saturday night the men would come in to town to spend their money in the hotels and it was like... how you say... a fête. We had Joe Frazier, the policeman, but what could he do with all these drinking men? So he just sat in the restaurant until all the fights were finished and the men fell asleep on the floors, then he arrested one of them and all the men from that company paid a dollar a week from then on to cover the damages." Caron shakes his head, "Like I say, a crazy time."

"Can you remember the night of April 12th, 1947, Monsieur Caron?"

"Oh oui, monsieur," Caron nods importantly. "That is the night my taxi was stolen."

Foss smiles. "Tell us about it."

"Well, this Boucher started to work at 8 p.m. and ended at midnight. I remember I was worried because the wind was blowing and it was beginning to snow. I went to my stand at midnight. Boucher is not back. Tissou, my other driver, tells me he has seen Boucher take a fare from the hotel down the block just after eight, but he does not know where they went." The memory of his anxiety quickens Caron's speech, jumbles his verb tenses. "Next morning still no Boucher. So I tell police my car is gone... I do not trust that guy."

"Why not? You hired him." Foss rocks back and forth again, his head poking forward, anticipating his next question even as he listens to Caron's answers.

"Yes, but already after only two days I have complaints he cheats the customer. Short changes."

"So you thought he had stolen your car and gone."

"Yes. But police say the road is very bad. Not one car can go by. So Tissou and I take the other two cabs on Sunday and go early, on the frost, to look—"

"On the frost?"

"When the road is still hard from the night. And I keep telling myself maybe Boucher is stuck in the bush someplace. I look all over, but..." Caron shrugs in remembered resignation.

"But eventually you found Boucher."

"Yes, on Monday. I was having my lunch in the restaurant when Constable Joe Frazier come for me and I identified my driver's body on the highway. He always wear the same thing, that one. Brown jacket, brown pants, and the boots..."

"Would you describe for us what you saw around the body?"

"Well," Caron looks at the ceiling, recalling the scene. "There was a wallet near the head. Constable Frazier kicked it with his foot, that is how we saw it under the snow. I remember this because it was empty and I say to myself, 'This can be no accident, then,' because I give all my drivers ten dollars to make change. Then there was the watch, a pocket watch."

"You have a remarkable memory, Monsieur Caron," Foss purrs. Caron stands up straight, his dignity restored.

"Now, did the police ever question you again, after that first day?"

"Yes. They find my taxi finally, in another town, I forget which. Then Constable Frazier showed me some pictures."

"Pictures? Of what?"

"Of men."

"I see. And did you recognize any of these suspects?"

"Objection." Cosselli is no longer bored. "My Lord, nobody has established that the pictures were of suspects."

"Sustained. The jury will disregard that."

"I beg the court's pardon, My Lord. I will rephrase that. Did you recognize any of the men in the pictures shown to you, Monsieur Caron?"

"No, sir."

Foss nods. "Now tell me, Monsieur Caron." Turning dramatically, he points at the prisoner, "Have you ever seen this man before?"

There is a pause. The prisoner clasps his hands firmly in his lap, trying to conceal the fright that has stilled every muscle in his face, as the taxi owner studies him. Then, incredibly, Caron nods.

"Yes, sir, I have seen this man."

The prisoner's eyes open wide. Cosselli's head jerks back. Throughout the courtroom there is a collective intake of breath. Foss smiles benignly.

"And can you tell us where that was, monsieur?"

Sensing his importance, Caron takes his time, concentrating. The courtroom clock behind me ticks off the seconds until finally he shakes his head.

"Excuse me, I cannot say for certain. But I do know this man from someplace in my life," Caron looks at the judge. "I never forget the face."

Bizarre wisps of memory, unexpected during a trial in which every move is pre-planned, can be dangerous. And here the francophone's misuse of a tiny preposition— "the face" instead of "a face"— adds immeasurable strength to the impression Foss has so painstakingly built in the jury's mind.

Defense counsel Peter Cosselli stands up slowly, waits a moment, then flashes a smile at the Crown's witness.

"Monsieur Caron, have you been interviewed by police about this case recently, say in the last month or two?"

Caron nods. "I sign a paper, yes."

"A statement."

"That is correct. I say what happened and a policeman write it down. Then I sign it."

"Right. So it would be fair to say that you have been thinking about this case more than usual in the last month or two, preparing to make a correct statement, to be a good witness?"

"Yes, of course. I want to help..." Caron begins to look wary.

"Of course," Cosselli smiles. "Now about your having seen Mr. Brown. You say you can no longer remember where or when it was that you saw him. That is understandable. These lapses, when a person looks familiar but we are not sure why, happen to us all. But can you remember whether you have seen him in person, or could it perhaps be a photograph that you recall?"

"No, it was his person."

"How can you be so sure, Monsieur?"

Caron's hands hold onto the railing around the witness stand. His eyes slide towards Foss. Having embarked upon a course, pride allows him no backtracking.

"I am sure."

"All right, then perhaps you will tell us roughly how long ago it was that you saw the accused? Was it a month ago, a year ago, five, ten years ago?"

Again Caron concentrates, trying so hard to hide his bewilderment, to find a proper, dignified way.

"I... cannot swear on the Bible," he says at last, "but I think... maybe it was not so long. Last summer? Or maybe last year?"

"Thank you, monsieur, for trying so hard on our behalf." Cosselli's voice makes clear how irrelevant is this man's desire to help.

Court adjourns at 6 p.m. Outside the curtains the rain has stopped. The streetlight at the corner glows red on the wet road.

I make it a habit to leave the courtroom last— the best clues to a story so often show themselves off-stage, after the dramatics. Now as the courtroom clears, Peter Cosselli sits reviewing his notes. I stop working on mine to watch Bertie, the old Scottish bailiff, come in to collect his prisoner. Cosselli waves Bertie away. The prisoner is left sitting alone for a few more minutes, then Cosselli comes slowly to his feet. Except for the two of them and me, the courtroom is empty.

Cosselli advances on his client, his black eyes pinning him now as squarely as if he were a butterfly on a collecting board.

"Rodger, is there anything, anything at all, that you have not told me?"

"What? No!" The man's voice is low, clear, sincere... a little too much so? Cosselli is watching him closely.

"You're sure? This afternoon they'll serve up the first cop. If there's anything at all about yourself, or about your dealings with the police that you haven't told me..."

The accused shakes his head. "No, there's nothing."

"Nothing about the night of the murder, in Geraldton?"

"No." But it comes out too fast, and now the man is looking away from Cosselli towards me. His face is handsome, finely sculpted, but a little seedy. His eyes are brown. His fingers play along the railing around the dock. Cosselli shakes his head, sighs.

Usually, after all the hours of interviewing, Cosselli can sense the inner workings of his clients' minds and then, invariably, he can see how they became enmeshed in the circumstances that have brought them to him.

There was the eighteen-year-old native, a shy, intelligent boy charged with the brutal axe murder of his uncle: an open-and-shut case, according to the police. The Crown had eye witnesses... But how, you had to wonder, could this boy have done such a thing? So Cosselli had gained as much confidence as the boy had been prepared to give, and then had listened. The family had been camping in the bush. The boy's mother, a crippled widow, was in charge of making the meals while the boy and his uncle, who was his mother's brother-in-law and a big man, twice the size of the boy, had hunted. One night after dinner and a few drinks, the uncle, a crude old bugger who stank of Four Aces, had begun to taunt her cruelly about her disabilities. Then he had advanced on her. The boy had yelled at him to stop. The uncle had laughed drunkenly, had swatted the boy out of the way. His mother had cried out. The uncle turned back to her, still laughing. And the boy, reeling back under the force of the blow, had spotted the axe propped in the corner of the tent...

Once Cosselli knew how tragedy had struck he could construct his strategy. The open-and-shut murder had been changed to manslaughter. The boy had been sentenced to ten years instead of life, would likely be out in three...

"This one's tough, though," Cosselli told me earlier, "Brown is a roustabout, but smart as a whip. Also..." Cosselli shook his head then too, "Six months I've been talking to him, and I still don't know it all..."

"Rodger," Cosselli tries one last time, "I get the feeling you're holding something back from me. If these cops come up with something you should have told me, the judge'll put you away. And you better hope he does, because if he doesn't, I personally will wring your scrawny neck."

"No, no," Rodger turns a wide-eyed look on his lawyer, and now I wonder.

They say he has come here looking for the truth. But if that is so, why would he hold out on his own lawyer?

Unless, now that he is caught in the clutches of the justice system, he has sensed how truth really figures in a court of law.

It took me until last winter, in darkest February when the northern sun sinks down over the mountains west of the city long before dinner and does not reappear until after breakfast, to see how the system works.

I was driving down the hill to the newspaper office scraping the early morning frost from my breath off the windshield in my Volkswagen, watching the red ball that was the sun rising out in Lake Superior, behind the Sleeping Giant, when the news came over the radio: the police had arrived at our plaza at 3 a.m. to find two young men scrabbling around the plaza's frozen parking lot, chasing bits of $10, $20, $100 bills. The Bank of Montreal's night deposit box was a black hole in the side of the building.

I laughed out loud. These were the psychedelic, Black Panther, Abbie Hoffman, money-is-bad days. Love— the thought of which brings such a sweet ache to my limbs— love, when finally you figured out how to live with it, would make the world a perfect place. Universal love would stop the greedy and the rampantly ambitious from ruining the world. So...

"Up the Revolution!" I cried that morning, revelling in the destruction of the plaza's temple to greed, and further clouding the windshield of my heaterless car.

But the two lank-haired brothers who stood before the judge later that morning were far too dim for revolution. "They were actually trying to rob the bank," Cosselli laughed, "and they weren't even doing it for themselves."

"Oh? For whom then?"

"The Choice. These guys' one goal in life is to join the Satan's Choice. The robbery was their initiation task."

"Oh, my God." I live alone in a basement apartment about six blocks from downtown Port Arthur. The Choice's local chapter headquarters is no more than a mile away. Their stringy ponytails and black leather swaggers, the jingle of the chains on their jackets, all of it advertising a freedom outside the law, terrify me. The only place for a woman in their world is under the heaving, sweating body of a man.

"So what'll you do?" I asked Cosselli. At least these two were caught red-handed.

"Oh, I'll pick my way through all the charges..." And so he had: the damage to a public place had been an accident because there had been no intent behind it, he argued. There had been no robbery because no money had been taken. Finally statements put forward by the Crown to prove attempted robbery were tainted beyond belief by the interrogating officer's playing on the brothers' fear of what the Choice would do to them for bungling. The judge had not bought all of it, but by the end of the day the brothers were on the street again.

I was stewing over a glass of draft in a Port Arthur bar with Barb Warner, our newspaper's Family Section editor, when Cosselli joined us.

"So," he raised his glass of Scotch. "To justice."

"Humph." I blew a stream of smoke up towards the ceiling.

"Oh, come on Claire, they'll get their come-uppance, if that's what's bothering you."

"Yeah, right. The Choice'll knife them and leave them to bleed to death in some miserable parking lot. Maybe jail would have been kinder, Peter."

Cosselli shook his head. "Those two aren't worth the price the Choice would pay for executing them. They'll suffer a beating maybe, and they won't get their memberships into the gang... until the next time the club needs them—"

"And some innocent bystander trying to do their banking gets blown to smithereens," said Barb.

Cosselli levelled one of his black-eyed looks at her. "I was just doing my job, Mrs. Warner, giving the accused the best defense I could under the law. Would you rob them of that?"

"No, of course we would not." I was darned if I would let him intimidate us. "But let's face it, Peter, the truth was—"

"Oh, I see, you know what the truth was. You're going to tell me you know exactly, precisely what happened in that parking lot? You were there?"

"They blew up the night deposit box, Peter, you know that."

"I do?"

"Oh, come on, the police said—"

"And you believe what the nice policeman said." Cosselli took another swig of his Scotch, poked a finger at me. "I'll tell you what, Claire. You go on sweetly believing that what the man in the uniform says is the Truth, and I'll hope you never happen to find yourself with one foot on the wrong side of the law. In the meantime I'll just deal with the court's rules about how the police can treat my clients when nobody is looking, before they 'confess.' Then I'll look at what the law defines as robbery.

"Did what happened last night fit that definition? Because whether you like it or not, Claire, that's all we've got to go on: rules and definitions." He took another drink.

"I do my thing, Foss does his, and hopefully, if we're both very good that day, something fairly decent will emerge. So," he raised his glass again, also an eyebrow. "To justice."

"Pompous ass," muttered Barb as Cosselli moved away.

I couldn't reply. I just sat there swirling my beer, staring into the circling tide of bubbles.

Something fairly decent. Not necessarily the whole truth. Because who knows what that is? Nobody saw the two dumb would-be Choice members blow up the deposit box that night. So were they guilty of theft? Or had they just happened along after the fact? What if the police had found a little old lady picking up the shredded money instead of two hoodlums?

I saw then that what people do, the chaos of human co-existence, was just like the swirling bubbles in my glass: a mass of actions and reactions, percolating, rising, exploding, in which the truth differs according to who is involved and which way you look at the facts you have. All justice does is lay a pattern of rules and definitions over top of the chaos...

If the evidence presented in a case is found to match the pattern called "Rape" or "Robbery" or "Murder," the accused person will be convicted. If not, he will go free. Innocence has little to do with it.

The thought brought me a picture of my father, back home in Ottawa. The owner of a construction company that builds houses as fast as the new flocks of civil servants arriving in the capital can afford the down payments, he hangs a Canadian flag over his porch every July 1st.

"Freedom is the key to everything," he has always told my brother and me, "here, you say what you want, go where you want. You have no idea how lucky we are."

But to what extent are we free, I wondered from the vantage point of my privilege? What if, in all innocence, you wandered into a web of circumstances you could not control, found yourself in the wrong place at the wrong time? And the police, thinking you were guilty, threw you into jail and made a case against you?

"Here you have recourse," my father would argue. "The whole story would come out in court!"

My mother, an Alberta girl whose family has farmed the Pincher Creek area for three generations, would just smile. She has an instinctive grasp of how wayward is the path of human endeavours. That's why she wishes I would please stop galavanting about chasing criminals, marry "that nice fellow I'm seeing," and be safe...

"I swear to you, Peter," the prisoner is saying now. "After all our talks you must know more about me than my own mother does."

Cosselli snorts. "That's not saying much." Cosselli signals to the bailiff, then, as an afterthought, to me.

"Come on over here, Claire. Rodger Brown, meet Claire McKeen, reporter for the Thunder Bay *Chronicle-Journal*. She will be telling your story to the world." Cosselli gives me a shark's grin.

"You don't have to worry about Claire, Rodger. I've known her for a couple of years now and you can trust her to be fair. So I've given her permission— subject to your approval, of course— to visit you during the trial, on the clear understanding that she will not publish anything you say until this is over. Is that okay with you?"

"Sure." The prisoner flashes me a grin. It is startlingly beautiful— white, guileless— an odd smile under the circumstances. I find myself smiling back.

"Perhaps I could drop by this evening?"

"Why not?" He shrugs. "I don't believe I have any other engagements."

The bailiff approaches, takes his charge's arm.

"Oh, by the way, Rodger," says Cosselli, "speaking of your mother, she's arriving in Thunder Bay tonight."

"No!" The humour drains out of Rodger's face.

"Now, come on man, you know your Uncle Arthur has to testify. I guess when she found that out, she made up her mind to come, too," Cosselli laughs, trying to lighten the moment. "You're always saying your mother has a will of steel."

"No, no, you don't understand," Rodger whispers. "She's not even supposed to know about this. For God's sake, Peter, she's seventy-seven!"

⊰ CHAPTER 3 ⊱

He is sitting in the small lawyer's room at the jail, gazing out the window into the dusk. The yard lamp goes on as I come into the room but Rodger does not appear to notice. The grey suit is gone, and sitting at the table in jailhouse denims, his back slumped against the chair, one of his legs splayed out under the table, he looks wrung out.

He startles as I close the door, hurries to his feet, comes around the table to pull out my chair.

"Please, don't bother," I smile, secretly tickled.

The walls in here are covered with the kind of green and white tiles somebody somewhere makes for public washrooms, train stations and jails. It is a lonely, soulless room. I keep my smile.

"So, what do you think of it all so far?"

"Pretty rough." He sits down, runs his hand over his forehead. "I never imagined..."

I nod. "I figured as much."

"I just thought I'd go to the cops and there'd be a trial right then and there, you know? We'd hash out all the stuff... I never dreamed that I'd have to sit here waiting for six months, twiddling my thumbs, playing chess with Clyde— who's a nice guy by the way, an extortionist waiting for sentencing— before the trial even started."

"You just missed the last Supreme Court assizes, I guess."

"Right. But do you know they won't even let me work? The others scrub the floors and the tiles in the common room, varnish the table," he shrugs, "it passes the time. But me, I'm not allowed to lift a finger because I haven't been found guilty of anything.

34

"So then why aren't I allowed out for a walk, to breathe some fresh air, buy some smokes, I ask? Because I might run away, they tell me. But I brought myself here, I remind them." He leans across the table towards me, "But you know what? They're right. They let me out and I'm not at all sure I wouldn't be long gone on the next train west."

I nod again. How can I blame him?

"Well," he sits back. "It serves me right, I guess. I should have known." Close up, he is seedy-appealing. Were he a successful member of the middle class, his thick wavy grey hair, warm brown eyes and straight teeth, the line of his nose and jaw, would have given him charisma. Instead, his history has drawn deep lines in his face, injected a kind of vulnerability no successful WASP knows into his eyes. It draws me. Brown is smart, Cosselli has said, but what else is he?

"How should you have known?" I offer him a cigarette, take one myself, slide my tape recorder onto the table between us. Take it slow, I tell myself. Do not smother him with your eagerness. "It's not as if you've ever been in jail before."

"Well, I guess when you get to be an old codger like me," he flicks my lighter, leans across the table to give me a light, "you should have an idea that things don't happen straight, the way you'd think they would." He cups his hand around the lighter flame, the habit of a man who has spent his life out of doors.

"I mean, look at the Bible. I read it a few times in the years after the murder happened. I thought maybe it could help me figure things out. But all it did was confuse the hell out of me...

"Take the story of Cain and Abel, for instance. They were the sons of Adam and Eve, right? The first humans to inhabit the earth. So there was nobody else around yet, right? But then it says that Cain slew Abel and went off into the bush and got himself a woman.

Well, where the blazes did he find this woman, that's what I want to know. I mean if his parents and Abel were the only other humans who existed..."

"Well, I guess you're not supposed to take the story literally." I can't help grinning.

"Yeah, well that's what I mean. Things just don't go straight, the way you'd think. But the question still remains. Cain got someone. So who was it?"

I shake my head, at a loss, thankful that my tape is picking this up.

"I finally decided he must have got himself an ape."

I burst out laughing.

"Well, who else was there?" He shrugs. "...So anyway, this trial's the same thing. I told them I wanted to sort this out, find out what happened at last: did I do it or not? Just get a straight answer. But it turns out there's no more straight answer for me than there was for Cain. So now here's my uncle having to testify, and my mother..." He rubs his forehead again. "Why couldn't she just stay home, take care of herself like most little old ladies? I told her I was going away to sea. Now if she has a heart attack, drops dead..."

"Does she know something? Maybe Foss wants her to testify."

"No, she knows nothing about any of it! And there's no way she's ever going to understand either. She never has." He looks at me and there, under the wrinkles and the grey wavy hair, is the fear of a small boy.

"Oh?" Is this a clue? "Will you tell me about her?"

"Well..." He glances at the tape recorder.

"I won't use any of it until later, after the trial's over and she's left. I promise."

He believes me. And I am right, she is a clue...

Once, when Rodger was five years old, he tells me, he left his tongue print in the ice cream their neighbours kept in an icebox on their back porch.

"Well," his mother asked him, her brown eyes boring into him. "Did you do it?"

"No!" he blurted, knowing she knew the truth, "It was Jessy, their dog, I saw her!" He ran from her eyes in those days. She chased him four blocks to give him a whipping. She was his greatest supporter, except when he was bad. "Then she turned into Mother Redemption."

Later, as a teenager back in Vancouver, Rodger sneaked out of the house in the middle of the night to go to beach parties with Charlie Dodds, smuggled a few bottles of beer out of the stack his father kept in the basement— perfectly normal teenage stuff. His father understood it. His mother did not even try to. Instead, when she found the empty beer cases one day while she was cleaning, her hard brown eyes seemed to reach right inside him, trying to cut that part of him— the fun part— out.

She loves you, his father told him once. And Rodger knows this, has always known it. One time, in September 1939, she even showed him.

Canada had just declared war. Charlie and Rodger were spending the summer washing dishes on the Princess Patricia, one of the coastal cruise ships.

"I'm gonna join up when we get home," Charlie, up to his elbows in soapy water, handed Rodger the last white dinner plate. "Think of it Rodg', Europe!"

"But you might get killed."

Charlie used the back of his arm to wipe the sweat off his face.

"Would you rather spend the best years of your life here?" Just above their heads grey pipes hissed and gurgled, hanging pots and pans chattered as the ship swayed on the sea swell. Salt and grease and stale food smells hung in the air. Except for the afternoons spent serving drinks on deck, their only contact with the sea, from six in the morning until dusk, was the one porthole over the sink. "A person could suffocate in here, Rodg'. Not me, I'm headed for The Fight!" Charlie let the greasy water out of the sink, raised a fist, "Freedom or death, that's where I'm headed!" he laughed. "Come on, let's go up on deck for a smoke."

Just then the swing door opened and one of the waiters, who apparently thought his black pants and red Princess Patricia waist-coat made him some kind of prince, came through with a tray loaded with a mountain of dirty dishes. "Here you are, boys."

Charlie's face fell. "Where did that come from?"

The waiter smiled down his nose. "Late sitting." He swung out again.

"Late sitting," Charlie mimicked.

Rodger looked at the tray, the porthole, then at the huge steel storage cupboards full of dishes. He started to laugh...

"We just dumped the whole tray— dirty plates, bowls, cups, knives, forks— out the porthole into the sea." Thirty-three years later in the Thunder Bay jail, Rodger laughs again. "We did it quite a bit after that. Some day four hundred years from now some archaeologist will find all the plates, knives, forks, glasses with the Princess Pat crest on them at the bottom of the Inside Passage, and he'll say, 'Hmm, now what kind of people would live at the bottom of the sea?'"

By the time the Princess Patricia docked in Vancouver, Rodger had decided to quit school and join Charlie. He was not quite eighteen.

"Why?" his mother demanded. "Charlie I can see. He's never going to amount to anything anyway, but you! You could finish school, make something of yourself. All the teachers say you're bright."

But it was too late. Dreams of England, France, of adventure, of leaving, had long since swept away any concerns about school or his future.

"There's a war on, Mother," Rodger tried. "Somebody's got to go, and who better than a young fellow with no attachments like me?"

"Don't you give me that, boy! There are plenty of others to serve as cannon fodder. Plenty who don't have to lie about their age."

"I'll be eighteen in three months."

"And a bigger fool I never saw."

The morning he was due to leave he came down to the kitchen wearing the Seaforth Highlanders' full battledress. Victor, his older brother, who worked with their father at the shipyard and had already left home, was coming to drive him to the armoury.

"Wow," breathed his little sister Jenny, seeing his uniform.

"You look like a real soldier Rodg'," said his younger brother Jimmy. "Can I try your cap?"

His father tried to chat, clearing his throat a lot while they drank coffee together. His mother, her slippers slup-slupping back and forth across the kitchen behind Rodger, said nothing at all. He had come down the stairs full of pride. Now he felt out of kilter, as if the uniform had given him a different shape so that even though this was the only home he had ever known, he no longer fitted in here. It was a terrible, sick feeling.

He got up, kissed little Jenny, took his cap back from Jimmy, shook hands with his father. His mother was standing at the sink, her back to him, but he could see how white her knuckles were as she held onto the edge of the counter.

"Mother?" He touched her shoulder, realized with a shock how small the bones were. And then suddenly, for the first time that he could remember, her arms came around him.

"Be so careful, son." Then she pulled away and he saw her tears.

She loved him, always had. So why, he wondered as the troop train pulled out of Vancouver station, was she so harsh?

A picture of his grandfather, old Hamish, her father, flashed into his mind. When Rodger was a small boy, the old man had come to stay with them once a year. Rodger remembered his long nose with the hairs sticking out of it and the black suit, always the black suit. He was a Mormon, had farmed down in the hills in southern Alberta; and Rodger's father kidded his mother that she had never seen a man other than old Hamish until her future husband had shown up selling tools and servicing vehicles. He had taken her for a ride in his car. Hearing about it at dinner, her father, a widower, had sounded God's own fury. When she had married Clive Brown, the old man had turned away to his Mormon prayers.

Years later, when age caught up with him, old Hamish relented, but still he tried to stand up for his God by lining up Victor, Rodger, Jimmy and even baby Jenny and reading long religious tracts to them. On and on he would read, and when the boys whispered to each other, trying to relieve their boredom, the old man would freeze them with a glare that Rodger recognized even then...

"The other thing I'm wondering," Rodger says now, more to himself than to me, "Is: if my mother knows what's going on here, does Elsa?"

"Elsa? Your wife, you mean?"

"No," he flashes a rueful smile. "Not yet anyway."

She is tall, he says, nearly his own height. Her eyes are blue, her hair crinkly, salt and pepper, her face freckled. He laughs. "The kind of face that tells you everything she's thinking."

"You love her."

"Yep, I do. This one's the one."

"Not the first, though?"

"Great Scott, no! At my age there's been all kinds of others, some I've married, some I haven't, but this one... Well," he looks at me, "you ever been in love?"

My jean-clad bottom squirms against the hard chair. "Yeah... well, I think so..."

"But you don't know." He nods knowingly, looks kind.

"Well there is someone... His name is John. He lives in Ottawa. We met at university, in the journalism school. He was two years ahead of me. Now he works for the government, but what he really wants is to edit his own paper. You know, a small, political, radical one, like I.F. Stone's in Washington..." Why am I telling him this? Am I really sitting in the jailhouse telling a man accused of murder the details of my innermost life? I feel myself colour.

"Ottawa?" He raises an eyebrow. "Isn't that kind of far away?"

"Well... no," I shift my boots under the table, "I save up the airfare, fly stand-by in the middle of the night. So does he. We get a weekend together about once a month."

"Once a month? Why don't you just go to Ottawa? There's a newspaper there, more than one... I'm sorry," he smiles, waves off the question, "it's none of my goddamned business, is it?... But once a month! Doesn't that kill you?"

"Yeah. It's not exactly ideal..." I find myself returning his smile. This is not something I can usually talk about. But here, locked away in this sterile, tiled little room, smoking cigarettes with no one watching, it's as if anything can be safely admitted. "John hates it, as a matter of fact. But I think things are pretty good the way they are. Well, safe, anyway... And I just have this feeling, like a warning bell, that maybe we better not change them."

"You like your freedom."

Freedom: drinking beer and dancing late into the night at the local pub, joking and laughing and warding off sweaty men to the tunes of Creedence Clearwater...

"No, it's not that so much... But here I live how I want, do what I want, write what I want. What I do matters. Not that he'd interfere at all if I were with him... but he might. Anyway I'd worry about it... About him trying to take control of my life, or not caring enough about it. Men tend to do both those things, you know."

He nods politely and I see that he has no idea what I'm talking about.

"I always thought that if you loved them, you married them," he smiles. "But then I'm an old-fashioned s.o.b."

"That's the way my parents think, too. 'If you love him, marry him,' says my mother, 'the rest will work itself out'... But the way I see it, that's a pretty big risk." I have not realized until this moment how the confusion has been squeezing me, that that is what makes me so snappish on Monday mornings after a weekend in Ottawa...

"See, my mother fell in love with my Dad and married him. And became The Wife, baking pies, sorting socks, raising the babies, prattling about life on the block while The Provider came home, read the newspaper, and made pronouncements that the rest of us accepted as truth. And my parents are happy enough in their roles— most of the time.

"But I wouldn't give you ten cents for my mother's life. Living with Father Knows Best would drive me clean out of my mind... I want to have babies and I want to be home for them, but I also want... I don't know," I look down at my purple and pink floral jeans and realize for the first time what I'm thinking: that love won't find me my path. "I guess it sounds like I want a lot."

Rodger chuckles, grinds his cigarette into the ashtray.

"You women— the good ones— are all alike. You go for a guy, tell him he's the one, the best. Then the next thing he knows, you're demanding more out of him..."

His last night in Vancouver, six months before, Rodger stopped for a drink on the way home from the shipyard. It was late April, his fifty-sixth birthday. Some of the boys were there and then someone spilled the beans about it being his birthday. One round led to another, but when he got home he was not blotto. And Elsa knew that he drank from time to time.

This evening her attitude was different, though, not just disapproving. There was uneasiness in the way she busied herself instead of looking at him, in her silence. She waited until the cake she had made him was cut, then she told him she was leaving him.

"No." He shook his head. She couldn't do that. She was the first woman in his life whom he could truly say he loved. He'd never really known what love was until he met Elsa. He had settled down here for her. They had been together nearly two years. "No, please Elsa, you don't want to leave me. Not on my birthday." He went to her, put his arms around her, "I'm sorry about tonight."

She said nothing, just stood there like one of those store mannequins. Suddenly, he was afraid.

"I'll do anything, honey. I'll stop drinking altogether—"

"It's not the drinking that's the problem, Rodger." She pulled away from him. Her eyes were light blue like the sky over the sea in the crisp, early mornings. But they were so hurt. "And it's not the nightmares that keep waking you up sweating night after night. It's what's behind them. Whatever it is, it's killing you, Rodger, why can't you see that?" She started to cry. "And as long as you go on refusing to tell me, to get it out once and for all, well I... I can't stand it!" She took a breath, "I just can't stand it any more."

So many times, in the night when she woke him and he found himself shaking, so many times he had wanted to tell her. Had very nearly done so.

But she was such a good person, such a beautiful, straight, warm person, better than he had any right to. She would have left him for sure.

He looked across the remains of the birthday cake at her. But now she was leaving him anyway. And she was so sad, he couldn't bear to see Elsa so sad.

He got up, kissed her on the cheek, put on his coat and left. And walking all night through an April sleet, the pain of her loss was a physical thing, agonizing, paralysing thought until, as the hours passed, the steady echo of his footsteps on the pavement soothed him, sobered him. The decision came to him just before dawn. When he got home, Elsa was sitting at the kitchen table in her blue dressing gown, drinking coffee. She looked so tired. Her hair had strayed out of control and he could see from the circles under her eyes that she had not slept. She looked all of her fifty-four years sitting there. He wanted more than anything to take her to bed, to snuggle down with her under the covers. Instead, he sat down beside her, took her hand. Told her the whole story.

She cried.

"You must go to the police, Rodg'. It's the only way."

"I know..." he nodded. "The only thing is... do you think you could wait for me, Elsa?"

She looked so sad. She nodded, shook her head, cried some more, and then finally looked at him in that straight way she had. "I don't know, Rodger."

He had not realized that night that he would have to come all the way back to Thunder Bay, that she would have to wait six months while he sat in jail because there was nobody here who could vouch for him, and the circuit judge only travelled north twice a year.

"I don't even know if she knows what's happened. Maybe she thinks I have been tried and found guilty, that I am a murderer rotting away in prison... Only please, dear God in heaven, don't let her have given up on me."

ᴄ CHAPTER 4 ᴐ

Rodger's mother, Margaret Brown, is sitting in the middle of one
of the courtroom pews, between Rodger's Uncle Arthur and Aunt
Bea. She looks small in her brown wool coat, dull– except for the
eyes. They glare around the courtroom at the wood panelling and
the red velvet curtains, at the spectators shuffling in. They must have
read this morning's newspaper. I concentrated on Chestleman and
Caron in my article, setting the scene, and did a colour sidebar on
the jury selection.

When the bailiff brings Rodger in, his mother's glare fastens
on him. Her eyes are brown, the same colour as Rodger's, but
hooded by age. Her jaw jutting forward is the prow of a galleon of
will.

I smile at him– we spent five hours talking last night– but after
one quick glance into the body of the courtroom, Rodger keeps his
eyes down, watches his feet moving one ahead of the other towards
the prisoner's dock.

At least the old lady is with Uncle Art and Aunt Bea. Although
they too look old. Uncle Art's powerful rancher's shoulders are coat
hangers under his suit and the broad grin Rodger has described is
absent. Art looks so... small. Aunt Bea is thinner but her round
face with its granny glasses is timeless and she did flash Rodger a
smile when he came in, bless her heart, trying to give him courage
across a distance that is so much wider than this courtroom.

"Detective Staff Sergeant Stanley Rudnicki!"

The sergeant is a polite, grey-haired Ontario Provincial Police
officer whose crepe-soled shoes have trod carefully, painstakingly
through every kind of human imbroglio.

"Detective, where were you stationed in 1947?" Foss is looking crisp this morning, his black gown newly pressed, his white wing collar freshly starched. Today, says the brisk stride he uses to cross from the lawyers' table in front of the prisoner's dock to the witness stand, he will build the case that will put his man away.

"At Hearst, sir. I was a corporal then."

"And do you recall the Boucher murder?"

"Yes, sir, I do. I was called in to investigate it by Constable Frazier at Geraldton."

Foss hands Rudnicki three eight-by-ten-inch photographs. "Do you recognize these, Detective?"

Rudnicki pulls on a pair of wire-rimmed spectacles and examines the prints.

"Yes, sir. They were taken by the Geraldton town photographer in April, 1947. See, there is his stamp on the back." Rudnicki's voice is relaxed, his words trimmed as neatly as his hair. "There was no police photographer in Geraldton at the time, so Constable Frazier took the town photographer with him to the scene. I saw these prints when I arrived from Hearst later in the afternoon on the day the body was found."

Foss turns to the judge.

"Your Lordship, both Constable Frazier and the town photographer have gone on to their just rewards. Staff Sergeant Rudnicki is the only man left alive who can identify these photographs as those of the deceased, also the only one left with a memory of the 1947 investigation. I ask that the court accept his identification of these photographs of the deceased."

The judge nods to Cosselli. "Any objection, Counsellor?"

Cosselli smiles obligingly.

"None, My Lord. We are all indebted to the sergeant."

The twenty-five-year-old black and white prints are the first grisly evidence of the corpse. Across from me, Rodger closes his eyes, rubs the bridge of his nose.

"Now, Staff Sergeant," Foss rocks onto the balls of his feet, "perhaps you will describe the wounds visible in those photographs?"

"Well, sir, there is a cut about two inches long above the right ear, and these darker patches on the hair and the ground around him are blood. That's not what killed him though. There is also a small hole in the right temple, barely discernible in these pictures... See, there." Rudnicki glances up, his glasses catching the light. "It was a bullet that killed him.

"We had the body removed, then later that afternoon Frazier and I returned to the scene to search for evidence. Half a mile east of the body I spotted some wires sticking up out of the snow. I pulled them up and found the taxi's roof light, you know those round cylindrical lights they used to carry just above the windshield.

"The next day our O.P.P. in Hearst found the taxi abandoned behind the railway station. The front seat covers were covered with blood and there was a bullet hole in the driver's door. Inside it they dug out a bullet."

"And what did you find out from all these exhibits, Detective?"

"We sent them to the R.C.M.P. crime detection lab in Ottawa." Rudnicki opens a file and reads from the reports written at the time. "The bullet came from a .38 calibre gun, probably a service revolver—"

"Just a moment Detective," Mr. Justice Harley looks down at Cosselli, "Mr. Cosselli, do you have any objection to the prosecution's tendering this evidence through Sergeant Rudnicki, even though the lab reports he is referring to were not filed by him?"

"No, My Lord," Cosselli comes to his feet looking earnest, "the defense is entirely in agreement with any means by which the constraints of time may be overcome in this rather unique case."

Foss shoots Cosselli a wary glance: why is he being so co-operative? The judge nods to the witness.

"You may proceed, Detective."

"The blood on the seat covers was type O positive, the same group as that of the deceased. The lab also found a clear, unidentified palm print on the roof light."

Across from me, Rodger frowns. The police in Vancouver took his fingerprints when he gave himself up six months ago, he told me so last night, but they have never taken a print of his palm. Not then, or all those years ago—

"Go on, please," Foss rocks forward. "Was there any other evidence found?"

"Yes, sir, there was a pair of pants. A switchman walking home for lunch the day after the body was found discovered them rolled up beside the tracks a few miles down the line east of Hearst. He brought them in to us the same afternoon. They looked as if they had just recently been thrown down there. They were mostly dry, in spite of the snow on the ground, except there was a large brown bloodstain on one leg."

"And did these pants bear any identification?" coos Foss.

Rodger closes his eyes. Cosselli will have told him on no account to show any feelings to the jury, so he must not know that his head is shaking as he waits for his mother to hear the first damning evidence of his betrayal.

"Yes, sir, they did. The label bore the name 'Brown.' We were able to trace them through the retailer to one Arthur Brown of Calgary, Alberta: an uncle of the accused. The pants were part of a two-pants suit."

Three or four jury members— the young mechanic in the middle of the front row, the middle-aged housewife and part-time teacher on this end of the back row— are staring at Rodger now, noting his reaction. Several others look dazed, unused to sitting still for so long, perhaps. One elderly man at the far end of the second row is nodding off to sleep.

"Now, Detective, you sent all your exhibits off to the lab. Where did your investigation go next?"

"Well, sir, Detective Inspector Richardson," Rudnicki gestures towards the phalanx of police officers sitting in the first pew behind the wooden railing, "not Inspector Allan Richardson, but his father, Inspector Gordon Richardson, came up from O.P.P. headquarters in Toronto to take charge and we started interviewing." Rudnicki glances at his files.

"There was the cab driver who had just relieved Boucher, and the manager of a gas station in Hearst, who was woken late on the Sunday night by a large French Canadian looking for gas for a '47 Mercury. There was someone— a thin man— sitting in the car. Then there was a shoe salesman whose .38 had been stolen..."

Rodger starts. He has told me about the shoe salesman, a pompous beachball of a man in a ghastly checked suit...

They met in a Winnipeg bar. Rodger, drifting on a cloud of cheap red wine at the time, stepped on the salesman's toes.

"Hey, watch the shoes!" the man cried, hopping on one foot. Tenderly, he wiped his shiny black dress shoe with his handkerchief, then smiled apologetically.

"Can't afford to mess up the merchandise, you know." He stuck out his hand, "Harvey's the name, shoes the game, heh, heh."

They told him they were travelling east and he offered them a ride as far as Geraldton.

"We'll split the gas, eh? Have a party. You can catch a train east from Geraldton..."

"And?" I asked Rodger, "did you go with him, catch a train east from Geraldton?"

"The bastard lied to us," Rodger looked at the top of the table in the green tiled visitor's room. "There were no trains east from Geraldton..."

"...But none of these leads took us very far," Rudnicki continues. "The shoe salesman's gun was found in the Paradise Tearoom icebox, jammed down behind some bottles of beer. We sent it, and all the other guns we found, down to the lab for comparison with the bullet we had found. We searched the lumber camps, the mines, we raided hotels and rooming houses to find the missing gun. We published the Frenchman's description in the *Globe and Mail* and alerted every police force in the province. We also kept interviewing people, and we took prints from various large French Canadians during the next few years, but none of it ever came to anything."

Foss is nodding slowly.

"Now Detective, let us turn the clock forward twenty-five years. How did you become involved again in this case?"

"Well, sir, I am now stationed at the Thunder Bay detachment. Upon receiving information from Inspector Allan Richardson of our Criminal Investigation Branch, on May 4, 1972, I charged Rodger Pearse Brown alias Jones with non-capital murder."

Foss nods again, reviews his notes, leaving a pause so that the words— 'alias Jones' and 'charged with murder' hang in the still courtroom air.

"Thank you, Staff Sergeant."

Rodger will be hearing the words through his mother's ears. They sound so low. *Alias:* a petty thief or purse snatcher. If only she could know that he had only used the name Jones once, the day he had gone to the police in Vancouver, to protect her from all this. I glance back at her. Her white arthritic knuckles are locked together, her lips tightly drawn. Then there are those hooded brown eyes that, fifty years after the ice cream incident, still seem to question whether Rodger is a liar...

Cosselli comes to his feet.

"Detective Staff Sergeant Rudnicki, may I too express my gratitude for your outstanding memory of this case," Cosselli smiles affably at the beginning of his cross-examination. "Without it, we should be stranded in a desert of ignorance."

Rudnicki has a whole career of experience taking cross-examination questions from lawyers like Cosselli. His answering smile holds no illusion about what is to come.

"I'm glad I can help."

"You will indeed be a great help, sir." Cosselli glances down at his notes, "Let us begin by returning to Mr. Brown's pants. Do you have a record of the lab analysis of the stains on them?"

"Yes, sir. The stain was blood, type AB."

"Type AB? You said earlier that the deceased had blood type O positive, did you not?"

"Yes, sir."

"Have you determined the blood type of the accused?"

"Yes, sir. He too carries type O positive."

"Well, isn't that interesting. The taxi driver and the man accused of his murder both had O positive blood. That means the blood on pants that once belonged to Mr. Brown was neither Mr.

Brown's nor Mr. Boucher's. It must have belonged to someone else entirely, is that not so, Detective?"

Rudnicki nods placidly. "That is correct."

There is no sound in the courtroom.

"Well, then perhaps you will tell us, Detective, what bearing pants stained with type AB blood can possibly have on a murder case in which both the deceased and the accused carried type O blood?"

"Well, sir, the facts that they were found so close to the scene just two days after the murder, and that they were owned by the accused, are relevant."

Cosselli nods. "Owned at some time or other by Mr. Brown, yes. But for all you know Mr. Brown might not have seen the pants for weeks. Did you not tell the court they were part of a two-pants suit?"

"Yes."

"And the pair you found had someone else's blood on them."

"Yes."

Cosselli takes a last glance at his notes, then leaves the lawyers' long table, heading towards the witness box.

"In any case, when you traced the pants to the accused back in 1947, what did you do?"

"We had him interviewed by the Vancouver detachment of the R.C.M.P."

"Ah, so now we begin to get all the facts out in this case. The accused was interviewed in 1947. Was he arrested then?"

"No, sir."

"Now Detective," Cosselli leans on the rail around the witness stand, "is there, anywhere among those 1947 reports of yours, a place where the name Brown occurs, other than in direct connection with the pants? In the report on that interview for instance?"

"Yes, sir," Rudnicki turns the pages in his file, "I believe there was one report... Ah, here—"

"May I see that, please?" Cosselli takes the page.

Foss bounds to his feet.

"My Lord, those are police files. Counsel for the defense has no right to anything that has not been duly entered as evidence!"

Cosselli looks at him, surprise written all over his face. The piece of paper from Rudnicki's file dangles from his fingers.

"But, My Lord, the detective has been reading these files into the record all afternoon." He looks at the page. "Now this appears to be a statement made by the accused to a Constable Lucas back in 1947, right after the murder—"

"My Lord!" Foss crosses to Cosselli, looking as if he is about to explode. "The records read in this morning concerned only the results of police investigations. Counsel himself agreed to admit them. But this," he snatches the paper out of Cosselli's hand, "this is only part of an incomplete record, and it has not been tendered as evidence. Counsel knows perfectly well that he has no right to it!"

Cosselli looks tolerant.

"If it please the court, My Lord, Mr. Foss was the one who raised the issue of the accused's pants, which fact places the accused in the vicinity of the crime. I therefore must contend that—"

"Gentlemen, that is enough," Mr. Justice Harley looks down at them over his bi-focals. "We will take a break. Court will reconvene at 3:30 p.m., at which time I will conduct a *voir dire*. The jury will therefore remain in the jury room until called."

A wave of murmurs crosses the courtroom. The jury members make perplexed faces at each other. The man on the end wakes up.

"What's happening?" Rodger asks Cosselli as soon as the judge has left. "What's a *voir dire*?"

Cosselli looks pleased with himself.

"It's a trial within a trial. Sometimes one side wants the jury to see or hear evidence that the other side thinks is legally inadmissible. So the jury is taken away while the two lawyers argue it out. The judge listens, then decides whether the evidence can become part of the trial."

"Oh." Rodger continues to look puzzled.

"What's at stake here is the statement you gave the police back in 1947." Cosselli smiles broadly.

"Yeah, that's what I don't understand." The day the police found him in 1947 Rodger was back home, at his parents' place in Vancouver. His mother ushered Constable Lucas into the parlour. There, among the mahogany and the doilies, the smells of stale air and furniture polish, and the picture of Christ that watched you no matter where you sat, he told Lucas he had sold the pants and gone east some other way. But...

"Don't you remember, I told you I made all that up. I didn't have any idea what I'd done and I was so scared..." He looks anxiously at Cosselli. "You don't want the jury to hear a pack of lies?"

Cosselli is still grinning. He claps Rodger on the arm.

"Don't you worry, sport. There's no way in God's earth we can win this *voir dire*. The jury won't hear any of it. Trust me."

I find the sergeant in the hall, drinking machine-made coffee out of a styrofoam cup.

"Those people you interviewed back in '47, what exactly did they tell you?" I ask him. Are there clues here that we have not heard in court?

No trial witness is ever allowed to testify to what another person has told them. Called 'hearsay,' this kind of second-hand evidence is considered unreliable. The information has to come into court from the source. But in this case the taxi driver and gas station manager are dead. Nobody knows what became of the travelling shoe salesman.

"Do you think I could have a look at the files?" I ask Rudnicki.

He is kind. "Sorry."

"Tell me then," I smile, pen poised over my notepad. "I'd rather hear it from you anyway. You were there. And I promise I won't use it until after the trial."

There is a pause.

"What harm can it do?" I venture.

"You will make it clear that this is not part of the trial?"

"Of course!"

"All right then, but this is strictly off the record until after there is a verdict. You do understand that..."

Tissou, the cab driver Boucher had just relieved, had been writing up his log in the taxi stand office when he heard a commotion, Rudnicki tells me. Someone down the block, outside the hotel, was calling in French for a cab. Glancing through the window, Tissou glimpsed a man talking to Boucher but the single bulb outside the shed's doorway cast a weak light and the falling snow further obstructed Tissou's view. All he could see was the silhouette of a large man in a light coloured coat. This man opened the back door of the cab company's blue Mercury and climbed in. Tissou did not notice whether anyone else got in because there were a lot of people around and the light did not reach beyond the near side of the cab. Anyway, he was more interested in his log. Boucher called out to him that he was going out of town and the taxi drove away.

Monsieur René Lamouraille, manager of a gas station on the outskirts of Hearst, heard a news bulletin asking for information about a blue Mercury the day after the body was found. He told

Rudnicki, back in 1947, that he was asleep late Sunday night in his house beside the pumps when someone banged on his door and called. He thought it must be an emergency. He looked out his bedroom window and saw a blue '47 Mercury. It could have been a taxi, although there was no light on the roof. The man at Lamouraille's door was very big, wearing a yellow Hudson's Bay coat and tall leather boots. He looked about thirty and spoke French. He wanted gas. The tank was empty and he was in a hurry. He gave Lamouraille five dollars and told him to keep the change.

Lamouraille had an idea there was at least one other man inside the car, maybe even two, smaller, thinner, but he could not swear to it. Nobody said anything while he filled the tank and Lamouraille was still half asleep.

"Lamouraille's description initiated a manhunt throughout Ontario," says Rudnicki. "Boucher was a drifter with no home, no close family or friends. Chances were his murderer had been a stranger to him, the motive robbery. But," Rudnicki shakes his head, chuckling, "as Monsieur Caron said yesterday, it was a crazy time. There were guns all over the place, most of them service revolvers left over from the war, many of them bought illegally or stolen from their rightful owners. We'd follow a lead round and round the mulberry bush...

"Take the shoe salesman who reported that a .38 had been stolen from the glove compartment of his car," Rudnicki continues. "He thought the three fellows he had driven to Geraldton must have taken it."

"He couldn't tell us much about these three, though. Apparently he was soon flying just as high as they were— but he did say that the one who had sat next to him in the front seat was a big French Canadian wearing a yellow Hudson's Bay coat and high leather boots. He said the man had curly hair and a large nose. The other two had spent the trip nursing a jug of wine in the back seat. The salesman thought these three had left Geraldton the day after arriving, but he could not say how.

"Well, it looked like our first break. Now we had a specific .38 calibre revolver to tie to the description of the Frenchman and his buddies. We redoubled our efforts.

"But a week later, a local stoolie came in to tell Constable Frazier about the gun in the Paradise Tearoom's icebox. The Tearoom, a local den of iniquity, was one of the first places we searched, but Constable Frazier went back and sure enough, there was the salesman's .38." Rudnicki shakes his head. "Another dead end." He lifts an eyebrow.

"Just like this statement they're making all the fuss about is a dead end."

"Your Lordship," Cosselli's face is bookish as he puts on his glasses, reads from his notes. "The defense submits that the document in question here is a copy of a typed statement the accused made to police in 1947. My investigation has revealed that a Constable Lucas, whose name appears at the bottom of this statement, is, like so many other witnesses in this case, no longer alive. I therefore suggest that because of the uniqueness of this case, the court must waive certain of its rules, just as we did in admitting the lab records as evidence. This is the only way we can scrutinize all statements pertaining to the accused. Denial of any evidence that could go towards establishing the innocence of Mr. Brown could result in a denial of justice.

"Is the accused, who has come here of his own free will seeking justice after twenty-five years, to be denied it because of the ravages of time? I beseech the court to rule in his favour."

The judge jots something down. "Mr. Foss?"

"My Lord, the ravages of time have nothing to do with this!" Foss is still angry. "What is at issue here is a copy of part of a policeman's report. There is no signature; it is not even the original document. There may have been a proper statement from the accused in existence once, but we can have no idea of the circumstances under which such a statement, if it even existed, was obtained. All we have here is an unidentified fragment of a police document, and I strongly object to my learned friend's 'beseeching the court' to order the police to give him any old piece of their records so that he can enter what suits him as evidence."

Rodger stares at the Crown attorney: what does it matter where the paper came from? Why is the Crown trying so hard to keep what he has said out of his trial? Foss cannot know it's all lies.

Mr. Justice Harley nods. It is not a hard decision.

"I'm sorry, Mr. Cosselli. There is no way I can allow a copy of an unsigned statement taken twenty-five years ago by someone who is now dead into court. Mr. Foss is right, we do not know the circumstances under which the statement was taken, or even, indeed, whether this is a statement." He looks hard at the defense counsel.

"You are usually the first person to insist that a man's rights be safeguarded in the taking of statements. So, what is going on here, I might well ask? But I will not waste the court's time. You are of course at liberty to enter the information contained in the document through your client later."

So it has all been a game. I have watched Cosselli often enough from my press table to recognize the signs: the lowered eyes, the apparent contriteness. Cosselli has known all along that the paper would not be admitted. Probably he didn't even want it admitted...

The jury files back in. Cosselli hooks a finger in his waistcoat pocket, continues his cross-examination as if nothing has happened.

"Sergeant Rudnicki, you have mentioned that Mr. Brown was interviewed during the course of the 1947 murder investigation. Was a palm print taken from Mr. Brown at that time, for comparison with the print taken from the taxi sign?"

"No, sir."

"Why not?"

"I cannot say for sure, but probably it was because Mr. Brown was not considered a suspect then."

"Oh, I see. He was not a suspect in 1947. The O.P.P. sent a man to Vancouver to interview him, and as a result of the information received at that time, he was dismissed as a suspect."

That's it, then. Cosselli has known all along that the statement will not be admitted. But he wants the jury to know that Rodger made a statement in 1947 and that the police do not want the statement read into court, that even though they spoke to him about his pants, the police did not consider him worth fingerprinting in 1947. He has used Rodger's lies as an invisible tool through which to discount the importance of the damning pants. Also, by instigating a *voir dire*, Cosselli has left the impression that the Crown is suppressing a statement made by the man they have charged. Not a bad afternoon's work.

But then wouldn't the pants have been dismissed anyway? The blood on them was obviously not part of this case... I glance at the jury to see what they are making of all this. The fireworks before the *voir dire*, followed by their break, has reawakened their interest. Even the Sleeper is sitting up straight now... Was that too Cosselli's purpose? I don't know whether to marvel or throw my pen down in disgust.

Courtroom games, dancing light-footed around the rules, have nothing whatever to do with a search for truth. As for justice? I know what Cosselli would say, he's told me often enough...

"Justice is what results, dear girl, what comes out at the end."

"Are you telling me the end justifies the means?" I waited, ready for a quote. "Are you saying the court is a kind of sausage factory where you squash and roll and stuff and twist the meat, and all the customer has to see at the end is his neatly packaged dinner? Never mind what's in it?"

He smiled at my outrage.

"I'd say it's more like an old-fashioned duel. The judge is the referee, making sure we stick to mutually agreed-upon rules. What positions we assume, the strategies we employ, those are up to the duellists."

I took a moment to think about that.

"So it doesn't matter what you do in the duel, how you conduct yourself within the limits? Whatever comes out is justice?"

"That's the theory."

"But what if one of the duellists is an excellent swordsman and the other one is slow and unco-ordinated? How can that duel deliver justice?"

"Well, just think about it." His smile was razor sharp. "What happens to a poor slow swordsman in his first duel?"

"But somebody's case was that first duel, Peter! How can you say he or she got justice?"

He smiled again.

"Do you have any idea how tough it is to graduate from law school? Those who do are supposed to be ready to make their living fighting duels..." But the analogy had fallen apart and he knew it. We both knew that the country's courtrooms are full of good and bad lawyers playing their parts in front of both careful, highly intelligent judges and grossly prejudiced or negligent ones. Who you get is a crap shoot.

"Look," he said finally, "the system is far from perfect, you know that. It's just the best we've been able to come up with so far."

"Maybe so. But heaven help the poor misbegotten joker who finds himself in the wrong court on the wrong day on the wrong side of the law..."

Love, I note for the second time in as many days, can't work unless we can all smell the roses...

"Now, Sergeant Rudnicki," Cosselli continues, "apparently the police did not fingerprint Mr. Brown in 1947. When you arrested him last November did you take a palm print to compare with the one from the 1947 investigation?"

"I couldn't do that, sir." Rudnicki's passivity gives no hint of what is coming.

"Oh? Why not?"

"I had nothing to compare it to. We can not find the record of the original palm print."

"You can't find the palm print?" Cosselli is incredulous.

"No, sir. The R.C.M.P., which was involved in the cross-Canada manhunt, says they have a record of sending the prints back to the O.P.P. in 1950. The O.P.P. has a record of having asked for the prints to be returned, but there is nothing anywhere to show that the prints were ever received."

There is a pause.

"You mean no one knows where the prints are?" The jury watches Cosselli's incredulity heighten. "Do you mean to say that two major Canadian police forces managed between them to lose a simple set of prints? This man's future depends on those prints,

Sergeant!" Cosselli takes a deep breath, expels it, regains his composure. "Well, never mind, there is still the roof light itself. Where is the roof light, Sergeant?"

Rudnicki blinks behind his glasses.

"Well, sir, after the investigation dried up in the early 1950s, all the exhibits were stored in the Geraldton police station... I understand they were then destroyed in 1968."

Another pause. Breathing ceases in the courtroom. Everyone— jurors, police witnesses, even me sitting safe behind my press table— waits for Cosselli, wincing at what will surely be a tempest of fury.

"Destroyed?" Cosselli whispers, as if he had no idea. "The Geraldton police took it upon themselves to decide that exhibits in an unsolved murder case should be destroyed?"

"Your Lordship, I object," says Foss. "This witness cannot be held accountable for the actions of the Geraldton police department."

"No, no, of course not," Cosselli shakes his head, "I beg the court's pardon. It's just that it would appear that the police themselves concluded in 1947 that the palm print belonged to the murderer. A simple comparison here today..." He gives a great shrug, sighs audibly, then returns to his notes.

"Sergeant Rudnicki, let us go on now to the gas station attendant and the thin man he may have seen in the car. Did you circulate this thin man's description along with that of the French Canadian?"

"No, sir, we did not. Lamouraille was not able to give us enough information."

"In fact, wasn't Lamouraille half asleep, and not even sure there was a second man in the car?"

"The information was vague, to be sure."

"Right, the vague idea of a sleepy man operating his gas pump in the dead of night... Let's try the shoe salesman's passengers. Did you circulate their descriptions?"

"No, sir. As I have said, his description of the men in the back was very vague and after the link with the gun was gone there was really nothing left to go on along that line of investigation."

"Nothing left. Right, that about sums it all up, doesn't it, Sergeant? Now, you mentioned that you have been involved in the present day investigation of this case. What have you been doing, exactly?"

"We went back to the place where the body and the other evidence were originally found, and searched the ground with a metal detector."

"Why?"

"Information newly received led us to look for the gun."

"And did you find it?"

"No, sir."

"Isn't it true, Sergeant, that in fact you do not have any physical evidence, any exhibits at all or even records of exhibits, that link this murder with the accused?"

Rudnicki looks straight at his questioner.

"That is true."

"And even though thin men may or may not have been seen twice with the suspected French Canadian, even though the accused was interviewed at the time of the original investigation, you did not suspect Rodger Pearse Brown of this murder until six months ago in November, 1972?"

"That is correct."

It is six o'clock. Detective Staff Sergeant Rudnicki has been on the witness stand all day. Tiredness has creased the skin around his eyes.

Cosselli thanks him, begins to sit down, then suddenly raises his hand.

"Oh, one more thing, Sergeant. Were you aware, at the time of the 1947 investigation, that another taxi driver had been beaten and robbed and left in the woods outside Port Arthur by three men on the same night as Boucher was killed at Geraldton?"

"I'm not sure..." Rudnicki thinks for a moment, then looks up, "but if that incident took place more than a hundred miles away at Port Arthur, on the same night as the Geraldton murder, it is surely doubtful that the two cases are connected? I do seem to remember that there was a rash of taxi driver assaults around then..."

"Quite so." It is Cosselli's turn to look benign. "Thank you again, Staff Sergeant."

When the cross-examining lawyer has finished tearing holes in a witness's testimony, the other side has an opportunity to mend the damage. Foss glances at the clock.

"Just one last question, Staff Sergeant. You have stated that in 1947 the police took an interest in Rodger Pearse Brown. Who reawakened this interest in him in 1972?"

Rudnicki nods towards the prisoner's box.

"The accused himself, sir."

Rodger is exhausted. He has been sitting still since 9 a.m., but he is evidently too tired even to taste the cold roast beef and mashed potatoes congealing on the plate his jailor has brought into the lawyer's room. He also looks afraid.

"Like I told you, I thought everyone would just stand up and say what they know, that the pieces of information would then fit together, like the tiles on these walls, to build up the truth, you know?

"But with all these questions and counter-questions, objections and *voir*-whatevers, it is more like they're building on quicksand. One lawyer no sooner gets the pieces neatly fitted together so you can see it all, than the other lawyer gets up and pokes and prods, and before you know it the whole thing has collapsed again..." He looks at me. "You can't stand up in quicksand."

I don't know what to say.

"How is my mother, do you know? Does she know I'm allowed visitors, I wonder?"

◄ CHAPTER 5 ►

People— retired couples, housewives, high school students whisper-
ing and giggling along the back row, anyone with a day to spare—
are pressed into the courtroom pews. Arthur, Bea and Margaret
Brown have to hold their coats and purses in bundles on their laps.

They can thank my newspaper stories for that. This morning's
headline would have jumped out at them from the newsstand in
the hotel lobby:

Sleeping Dogs Woken in 25-Year-Old Murder Trial

Uncle Art is staring at me. He is cut from the same mould as
Rodger— slim build, wavy white hair— but age has turned his
shoulders into coat hangers. His mustache moves as he chews over
his worry.

Damn media, I can see him thinking, why can't they leave a
man to settle his affairs in private?

Later, after the trial, Art will tell me that he and Bea tried to get
Margaret to stay home in Vancouver. What good could she do
Rodger here? But she insisted on coming— an angry old hen
standing by one of her brood. So last night he asked her if she would
like to visit Rodger.

She shook her head, one short jerk, her lips tight. It shocked
Art at first. Then he noticed her hand, how it was clinging to his.

"Come on Marg'," he put his arm around her, "we'll get you
settled. I've got a flask," he whispered, "I'll get some hot water and
make you a toddy, okay?"

She isn't really such a tough old nut, Arthur says. He remembers when his brother Clive brought her down to the ranch on his way through Calgary just after they married. Her father's acreage, down in southern Alberta, in Mormon country, had been so far back in the hills that sometimes during winter blizzards they could not get off the farm at all, not even to go to the tabernacle.

At that time Clive worked as a mechanic, selling and servicing farm machinery and the new automobiles, building, with the quick Brown smile and his ready wit, the reputation that would eventually secure him a future at the Vancouver shipyard. Old Hamish's farm was one of his regular stops and Arthur could easily imagine Clive tossing comments to this shy, duty-bound prairie girl, making a bet with himself that he could loosen her up, make her laugh. The bet brought him far more than he ever could have foreseen. For the shy, serious girl whose dark eyes gave nothing away, turned out to be beautiful: so innocent and delicate, so... good.

"And what about old Hamish, how did you soften him up?" Arthur asked Clive over a rye and ginger.

"I didn't. Nothing in this wicked world of ours will ever soften up that miserable old warhorse. So finally I just asked her without telling the old fart," Clive laughed, "and damned if she didn't say yes! Defied him outright, and came away with me."

"You eloped!"

"Yep, but don't get me wrong, we married right away, the same day," Clive looked into his drink. "She's going to be good for me, Art. She's the one."

Later, after they had been playing cards and Margaret had tasted rye for the first time in her life, Arthur saw the light come into her dark eyes. It changed her from a quiet, mysterious person into a sexy, irresistible mass of giggles. Clive had to carry her up to bed.

Arthur and Bea didn't see them for several years after that, by which time tramping up and down the country with four babies in tow— for she never would leave Clive's side— had begun to leave its mark. The light came into her eyes less often. Margaret began to turn dour like her father, as if having once defied him, she must now become his disciple. Or maybe it was the only way she knew to be a parent. Maybe she thought that truth, righteousness were all that she had to give. Whatever her reasons, the upshot was that her own children never saw the way her eyes could dance.

And now Clive is gone, cancer from the fumes in the shipyard boiler room, according to Margaret. All she has left are her children.

I glance at her now, sitting beside Arthur in the courtroom pew. Her gaze is fastened on the door at the front of the room.

It opens. The noise level in the courtroom drops as Rodger comes through but, smiling at a joke with the bailiff, he does not appear to notice the crowd.

It's a ruse, of course. Underneath the grin I can see the strain on his face even from here, the dark circles under his eyes.

"Arthur Brown!"

Bea reaches over to squeeze Art's hand. He walks stiffly, listing only slightly to one side, up the aisle, past my press table. Then he is facing the court, swearing on his honour...

Everything looks so different from up there, he tells me later. The judge and the lawyers, all these black gowns, are so close. He looks for Bea in the body of the courtroom. A sea of faces stares back at him. He tries to smile across at his nephew, sees Rodger trying to smile back.

"Now, Mr. Brown," Foss begins. "You are the accused's uncle?"

"That's right, sir." And proud he is of it, too. But there seems to be a frog in his throat. His voice sounds old and gravelly. He tries to clear it, squares his shoulders.

"And you have known your nephew all his life, Mr. Brown?"

"That's right. When they were boys Rodger and his older brother Victor used to come out to the ranch help in the summers. Bea and I—" Arthur stops. Don't volunteer anything, Cosselli has told him.

"Yes?" Foss smiles a viper's smile. "What kind of a boy was Rodger, sir?"

"Oh he was a good boy: polite, friendly, quick as a whip when it came to learning anything."

"A smart boy," repeats Foss. "Was he a hard worker, too?"

"Sure he was," Arthur smiles a little, recalling the fence-mending expeditions when Victor and Rodger would take a picnic and ride out onto the range. It would be nightfall by the time they returned. The fences had been mended, but who knew what else they had been up to out there? Hard work wasn't the point... "He's a fine boy."

"Reliable?"

"Your Lordship," Cosselli pushes himself to his feet, "surely the Crown can find better grounds upon which to base his case than how the accused performed his chores as a boy."

The judge raises an eyebrow at the Crown.

"Mr. Foss?"

"My Lord, I am simply establishing background in terms of character..." The man's voice drones on, but Arthur pays no attention. His aged mind, I can see, has skipped back again...

Reliable? The smells of roasting turkey and burning leaves come to Art with the memory of a crisp autumn Thanksgiving, when he and Bea visited the family in their big old frame house in North Vancouver. This was the first year that Rodger did not come to Calgary for the summer. Instead, he and his friend Charlie Dodds spent the summer working as dishwashers on a coastal cruise ship. They must have been about sixteen. And as Arthur, Clive and the boy sat out on the veranda, drinking a beer before dinner, Rodger regaled them with stories about the rich American passengers:

"Harry, Harry, look at that white stuff on the mountains!" The voice of a blue-haired woman from Los Angeles shattered the blue-green afternoon. "What is that stuff, boy?"

"The white, Ma'am? Why that's angel poo."

"Naw, yer puttin' me on! Really?"

"No shit, Ma'am— begging your pardon."

Reliable? Well... as Cosselli has just said, how relevant is any of this, anyway?

"...Very well." Foss must have lost the argument. His voice is acerbic. "Mr. Brown, perhaps you would tell the court when you stopped seeing the accused regularly, every summer."

"Um. I would guess that must have been in the late thirties. Rodger worked on a cruise ship for a couple of summers, then in the fall of '39 he went to war."

"And when did you see him after that?"

"Well, that would have been in about '44. He came home badly wounded. The army gave him six months' convalescence leave before his discharge and he and his wife Margaret came down to spend the time with us."

"Oh, so he had married. When did that happen?"

"It was during the war. She was an English girl."

"It's a strange thing, hearing people talk about you as if you weren't there," Rodger tells me that night. "It's a bit like watching yourself in a movie... only so much of the action— and all of the feelings— are missing."

He met his wife in December of 1942, his third perishing winter in a Britain short of coal, food, arms, everything. Invasion was thought to be imminent and every citizen from schoolboys to little old ladies was saving bottle caps, even collecting baskets full of stones. And still there was no sign of active duty for the Canadians.

The Seaforth Highlanders were stationed on the south coast, just north of the seaside town of Brighton, and one day Rodger went into the Brighton post office with a Christmas card for home.

"Fancy, another wild Canadian." The girl behind the post office counter eyed the red patch on his shoulder. "Honestly, I don't believe there's an Englishman left in Brighton." Her grey eyes had laughed at him. She had wavy light brown hair that tumbled down to her shoulders and a slightly pointed tomboy's face that moved easily into a smile. Rodger couldn't think of anything to say. His experience with British women to date had been confined to the safe barroom banter of women used to spending their time there. This girl was from the other end of the universe. Her laughing eyes were free of pretence or guile or anything other than humour. They were beautiful.

"Shall I weigh that, then?" She pointed to the letter lying forgotten in his hand.

"Oh. Yes, please."

"What's your name?"

"Brown. Rodger Brown."

"Well, Mr. Brown, that'll be sixpence please."

Heavy British coins clattered onto the counter as he fumbled for the right change.

"Where're you from, then?" she asked.

"Vancouver. On the far side of Canada, on the Pacific."

"The Pacific, fancy! That is a long way away."

She was obviously impressed. Rodger relaxed a little, leaned an elbow on the counter and smiled. But then the door opened and a chilly draft ushered in a clutch of customers. They lined up behind him. He would have to do something. Now. Or else risk losing the ground he had so unexpectedly gained.

"Your name! What's your name?"

"It's Maggie. Margaret Landry."

"Margaret, that's my mother's name too," he smiled. "Would you care to meet me after work, Maggie?"

"I can't, not tonight." But her eyes returned his smile. "You could ask me about tomorrow though."

A salt sea wind was howling in off the English Channel at dusk, emptying the streets as they battled their way up the hill to Margaret's neighbourhood pub. They shed their coats and settled at a corner table where the pub air, heavy with a damp beery warmth, closed around them.

Rodger asked her about the post office. She told him she'd been there three years, since leaving school.

"I wanted to join the WRN's, you know, join The Fight— but they said I was too young."

"How old are you?"

"Nineteen, now," she looked at him, "how old are you?"

"Twenty."

"You're young too, then. Anyway, I imagine I shall try again, to join the WRN's I mean. In the meantime I do firewatching, blackout patrols."

"That's dangerous, isn't it?"

"Well, of course it is," she laughed, surprised. "But everyone does it. It's quite exciting really, sitting up there on the post office roof in the dark, with our sand and our stirrup pump..."

Rodger nodded. Sometimes on a moonlit night you could see the firewatchers' silhouettes moving like night spirits across the rooftops to extinguish the little fires, lit by German incendiaries, before they could grow into flaming targets for larger, lethal bombs. But that was not the danger he had in mind.

"What about walking around the town on patrol in the middle of the night, aren't you afraid?"

"Of what?"

"Oh, I don't know," he looked away from her. "Drunken soldiers?"

"Oh, no, heavens no!" she laughed. "I never thought of that. We go in twos... And I can't imagine anyone attacking a blackout patrol. It would be so... unpatriotic!" They both laughed.

"So, now tell me about you."

"Me?"

"Yes."

Rodger shrugged. "You already know it all. I'm a soldier from Vancouver, Canada."

"Oh, come on," she laughed. "There must be more than that. What will you do after the war, for instance?"

He shrugged again.

"Who knows? I can hardly imagine life without war any more... And yet even after all these years, all the training we've done, there is no war, not for us anyway..."

Her smile was sympathetic.

"Tell me about Vancouver then, about the Pacific Ocean. I've been to London once or twice to see my aunt, but that's as far as I've ever been."

So he told her about Stanley Park and Horseshoe Bay, about the huge gulls, three times the size of her British ones, about his family and the old wooden house in North Van, how it always needed painting, about the view from the top of Grouse Mountain, about Charlie and their joining up, and he had never talked so freely to a woman before in his life.

They married in the spring of '43 and spent three idyllic days in a cottage Maggie's aunt lent them on the Downs near Lewes, and he sat with his bride on the front step that first night, watching the sun sink behind the hills to the west, while to the east a full moon rose to take over the night stage. In the trees and hedges around them birds called out their evening songs, drummed their wings, boasting about courtship. He slipped his arm around Maggie's waist, felt her move close against him. She was not the first woman he had lain with, but this was so different. She was his wife. For life. Excitement, fear, arousal, apprehension coursed through him all at once. The sky darkened, the stars taking their places like bit players on a stage that was centred right here in this garden. Rodger turned to her, kissed her hair, her forehead, found her lips...

The next morning he awoke to find her still sleeping, her breath soft against his shoulder. He could not believe his good fortune. He wanted to take her into his arms again, to press his whole body down onto, into her, to feel her all around him. Instead he leaned over gently, trying not to wake her with his kiss.

"You'll never be sorry, Mrs. Brown," he whispered.

Her eyes flickered open. Then she reached up, traced the curve of his cheek and smiled.

"Promise?"

A month later he was sent into action. As gun sergeant in charge of a six-pound anti-tank gun and four men, he was bound for Italy. Charlie was his corporal.

Maggie cried when he kissed her goodbye. He hugged her, nuzzling her hair, but he felt guilty. He loved her with a pride few men could know. But he was also excited as hell. After four years of waiting, he was finally going to see action. He was twenty-one.

"I'll be back," he wiped her tears away. "You wait, I'll be home again before you know it."

Six weeks later he and Charlie were stretched out on a dusty Sicilian hillside, resting up for that night's attack on Leonforte, a citadel built on the lip of Sicily's Mount Assora, when suddenly something moved in the brush of a dry ravine below them.

Rodger snatched up his tommy gun, flipped over onto his stomach, his mind listing the possibilities as he searched the brush.

"What is it?" Charlie opened one eye.

"Shsh!"

There it was again: a branch jiggling. Rodger took aim, pressed his finger against the trigger.

A tiny hand waved at him from the top of the bush. Then a small black-haired head appeared.

"No, Signore, please!"

A second head, even smaller, and inhabited by two enormous brown eyes, appeared. Then a boy, about five, came out from behind the bush. Clinging to his hand was a tiny girl in a dust-coloured smock. The boy's chin was wobbling.

"Kids!" Charlie cried. Rodger put down his gun.

"Christ, will you look at them though, they're terrified."

"What the fuck are they doing out here?" Charlie looked around anxiously. "They could get killed."

"Come here," Rodger motioned to them, smiling. "I won't hurt you."

They did not move, but their eyes fixed on his smile. Slowly, Rodger reached for his pack, found an army issue chocolate bar. He held it out, still smiling, "For you."

The little girl's brown eyes moved sideways to see what her brother would do. He looked doubtfully at Rodger's hand, at his smiling face, then back at the hand. Rodger motioned toward his own mouth.

"Yum, good. *Buono*. Here, I won't hurt you."

Cautiously, still holding his sister's hand, the boy took a step forward, another, until reaching out he could snatch the candy. He broke a piece off into his mouth. The grimy face broke into a grin. The little girl's fear fell away.

"Some for me, Carlos!" the little girl demanded in Italian as she bounced up and down, "Carlos, some for me!"

That night the Seaforth Highlanders threw wave after wave of men up the Leonforte hill against the pounding guns of a German Panzer unit. Rodger watched many of the men he had spent the last four years with being brought back down with their legs and arms and heads dangling from blood-soaked stretchers, while overhead the darkness was exploding with the sounds and smells of hell, and as he watched, anger began to replace his fear, so that when he could see the shells of his six-pounder smashing through the enemies' red-tiled roofs, exploding right on target, he whooped as loudly as the others. The battle on Bloody Hill lasted two days. When Rodger's carrier finally rumbled into the town, the Sicilian survivors were emerging like mice from the cellars, the children scrambling through the rubble while their elders wept and wailed or silently dragged out their dead.

A ray of the harsh Mediterranean sunlight lit on a dust-coloured bundle of rags just inside an alley. One tiny sunbrowned leg protruded.

Rodger jumped down from his carrier, ran into the alley.

She was lying face down, the back of her little head shot away. Gingerly Rodger turned her over. Her brown lifeless eyes stared at him. Bits of sand were stuck to the side of her mouth. Rodger brushed them away. Minutes went by but he did not know it, could not break the stare of that beautiful, grubby little face that was still as stone, and his own words kept crooning cruelly back to him through a fish-eyed memory of his smile: "I won't hurt you..."

Then Charlie was squatting beside him.

"She's gone, Rodg'."

Out on the road their army was rumbling by. Charlie looked up and down the alley. They were not covered here. He touched his friend's arm.

"There's nothing you can do for her, buddy."

Rodger looked up, caught a movement in the shadows against a wall: the boy. Hatred gleamed in his five-year-old eyes.

All through the next day and night the Seaforth Highlanders and the Panzers fired volley after volley at each other, decimating the sparse Sicilian hillsides, shaking the bright sun-parched air with explosions, bursts of machine gun fire and the cries and shouts and the moans that are war, and lying in a trench was like lying in a hot, smoky hell.

Rodger and his men were sprawled on the grass eating hardtack when a whistle sounded nearer than usual. Then came the thud: explosion. Rodger ducked his head. The second whistle was nearer still.

"Better get down boys," called Rodger. "They're getting awful close."

The thud came just as the men hit the trenches, then the flash, then an earthquake.

There was no pain. It wasn't until he looked down and saw his arm, then the huge piece of shrapnel sticking out of his gut that he knew he was hit. Then the weakness came, obliterating everything...

"Would you say, Mr. Brown, that the war experience had any effect upon the accused?" Foss is asking.

"Oh, definitely, sir," says Uncle Art. "He was in hospital in Algeria and then England for six months. Then when he came home they did more surgery. By the time he came to us nearly a year later he was still as weak as a kitten..."

"The shrapnel took a piece out of your arm, and most of your stomach, Rodger." The nurse's lipsticked lips, a cheerful banner, came towards him through the haze. "Also, Doctor says your intestines are a bit of a mess. But we've fixed you up for the moment with a colostomy and..." her voice faded as something else tugged at him, something out in the border regions of his mind. He frowned, concentrating, saw a small dust-coloured bundle. The pain stabbed him, he sobbed... But this was not it. He moved on through the muck and the dust and the moaning, blood everywhere, and the dying, to a dusty hospital tent, sorrowful faces leaning over him, telling him—

"No!" he tried to sit up, shaking his head, "no, no, no!" Fell back as the pain shrieked through his body, seemed to tear him open, "Charlie!"

August was giving way to September when Rodger came around for good. He found himself in a quiet, high-ceilinged room. Beds jutted out from the walls like tiny quays, strange metal apparatus moored to some, including his own. Beyond the tall arched windows he could see a cloudless Mediterranean sky.

He experimented with moving. Fingers, hands, arms: sore, but okay. Toes, feet: check. Legs: no. And not torso! So, he must not move. Why not?... Would he ever move?

In the bed next to him a boy with blond hair was reading aloud to himself in a quiet voice. It sounded like a litany.

Just what I need, thought Rodger, a goddamned holy-roller for a neighbour, telling me all this is God's will. Well, hallelluya, brother, save yourself, not me. He turned his face away. Passed the time by making animals out of the maze of cracks across the ceiling: a snake.

Too easy.

A duck then, there... And a bear! An honest to God British Columbia grizzly, complete with the muscle-bound hump over its forelegs, was stalking the duck...

The whisper beside him droned on. Curiosity finally got the better of Rodger. He turned his head back to the boy.

"What's that you're reading?"

"Hey, you're awake! I can't believe it, you want me to call the nurse?"

Nothing about God Be Praised. Rodger smiled.

"Nah, I'm okay for now. What're you reading anyway?"

"Oh, this." The boy looked down at his book. "It's poetry."

"Poetry!" Rodger started to laugh, caught his breath as the pain ripped through him, "Poetry?" His only exposure to poetry had been a high school dissection of the "Ode to a Grecian Urn." Poetry, he had learned, had no place in the life of a teenager.

"This is great stuff," insisted his neighbour, "I found it in the hospital library. Just listen to this." And before Rodger could object,

his neighbour had turned on his side, propped himself up on one
elbow:

Wild and wide are my borders, stern as
death is my sway,
And I wait for the men who will win me—
And I will not be won in a day...

Rodger found himself swept up by the rhythm, then the words.
He listened for the rest of the morning, then borrowed the book,
abandoned the duck on the ceiling to the bear in favour of:

The strong life that never knows harness;
The wilds where the caribou call;
The freshness, the freedom, the farness—

The rolling rhythms of Robert Service's Yukon poetry and the
pictures they painted soothed him for many months, helped him
escape the spasms clutching his belly, the little girl's dead eyes and
her brother's hatred... the memory of Charlie's death. Someday
Rodger would go to that Yukon.

"So you saw the accused and his wife in 1944," Foss continues.
"Did he recover fully?"

"Oh, yes, in a manner of speaking. He spent some time in
hospital in Vancouver as soon as he got home. They rebuilt his
stomach and removed the colostomy. Then when he came to us,
Bea and his wife Margaret filled him full of home cooking, whatever
he could eat, and after a while he got pretty near fit as a fiddle. They

left us in the fall to settle in Vancouver, and Rodger went to work as an apprentice in the shipyard, where Clive was."

"And after that when did you see them again?"

"They brought their first baby down. That must have been about a year later."

"And after that?"

Uncle Art's hands begin to flutter along the top of the railing. "I... I'm not sure I can recall exactly."

"Well, did you return to your habit of seeing them every year?"

"No, not every year. They had another child..."

"Well, let's try it another way, Mr. Brown. When did you stop seeing your nephew and his family on a regular basis?"

"Oh... I guess that would have been two or three years after the war... I'm not sure exactly."

"Why did they not come to see you any more?"

Uncle Art looks at his hands.

"Margaret left him."

"His wife left him? Did she take the children?"

"She took one and left the other, but she came—"

"Just answer the questions please, Mr. Brown. What year would that have been?"

"Well, as I said, I... don't rightly recall."

"Well, was it still the 1940s? Was it '46, '47, '48– ?"

"Objection!" Cosselli barks, half rising at the lawyers' table. "Counsel is badgering."

"Sustained." But Mr. Justice Harley leans towards Uncle Art. "Just tell us what you yourself know, Mr. Brown."

"Well, sir, the truth is that I don't know. It's all a long time ago now... It was shortly after the war. That's all I can say for certain."

Rodger risks a smile: hang in, Uncle Art.

Back in the body of the courtroom the little old lady with the granny glasses smiles, too. Foss takes another tack.

"You were fond of your nephew Rodger, were you Mr. Brown?"

"Oh yes, sir, very fond."

Foss rocks forward.

"And did you ever, during that troubled year shortly after the war, see the accused alone at your ranch?"

There is no way out of that one.

"Yes, sir, I did."

"What was the occasion?"

"Well, sir, as I have said, he and Margaret had had... some kind of trouble and she had left him to go home to England."

"I see. And what did the accused do then?" Foss is smug.

"He followed her. And I guess he was in something of a hurry," Uncle Art tells the court, "because when he arrived at our place he looked as if he had been struck by lightning. He had crossed the Rockies in a reefer."

"A reefer?" Foss asks.

Rodger smiles in spite of himself. What would Foss know about reefers and riding the rails? His mind drifts back, as it did during my visit last night, to Kamloops Station...

The dry afternoon wind rattled a roll of tumbleweed brittle as witch's bones against Rodger's legs as he crouched behind a disused boxcar, his eyes moving slowly down the waiting train until he saw what he was looking for: a break in the wall of a car— an open door.

He sprinted down the line, shifted the door a little wider and hoisted himself up and in. A moment later there was a bone-jarring jolt and the boxcar began to roll. Rodger crawled out of the draft from the door, wedged his pack against the vibrating wall behind him. But it was so cold in here, even colder than outside.

The train picked up speed and began to climb, snow-covered pines flashing by the open door like abominable snowmen watching a parade. Cursing the cold, Rodger put on all the clothes in his pack, but still the icy fingers crept relentlessly under the layers of cotton, wool, found his flesh, went through to his bones until even his blood ached.

He stood up, lost his balance as the car swayed, and reached out to steady himself against the wall. His fingers stuck to it.

Oh sweet Jesus, he was in a refrigerator car! And there were no stops before Calgary, on the other side of the mountains.

The train twisted higher and he began to freeze. First his feet. He took off his boots, blew into them, rubbed his toes, but now his hands weren't working very well. He could no longer feel his fingers. What to do?

His mind began to cloud over... Maybe he would die in here...

"Do not allow the victim to sleep," barked a familiar voice. Rodger started, looked around for the source.

"The internal organs will freeze and once the body temperature goes below..." It was the sergeant back in England, preparing them for action... in Sicily.

Rodger giggled and it was as if the sound, hearing itself, grew louder, shriller.

"Shut up!" Hearing his voice cheered him. He sat up straight, and began to sing:

"Way down upon the Swanee River..." He sang all through the night, all the way to Calgary.

Uncle Art might not remember the date but Rodger certainly did. It was April 4, 1947— nine days before the murder.

"He stayed with us for several days," Uncle Art continues. "We talked things over, settled his plans."

"What about his job? Did he take holidays to make this trip?"

"He had just come off a ship."

"But he was still an apprentice at the shipyard?"

"Oh..." Uncle Art shrugs, "I'm sorry, I don't know much about that... They sometimes did stints at sea, I think."

Foss nods. His voice when he speaks again is very serious.

"Obviously, if he arrived in a reefer, he did not bring with him the child his wife had left him."

"No, sir. Little Rodger was a brand new baby. Margaret, my nephew's mother, had him, and Rodger expected to be back very soon with his wife Margaret. He thought, you see, that if he went after her, showed her—"

"Never mind what he thought, Mr. Brown. When he left you to continue east, did you give him anything?"

Uncle Art looks at his hands.

"Answer please, Mr. Brown. Did you give the accused anything?"

"...Yes."

"Speak up please, sir. Describe for the court just what you gave the accused."

"We gave him a train ticket east as far as Winnipeg. From there he could apply for day jobs in the mines or logging camps, to pay the rest of his way."

"Anything else?"

"Well... we gave him a suit, one of my brown tweeds, with two pairs of pants... He wore one and carried the other." Uncle Art looks at Rodger, his face full of a new idea, "And now I'm thinking that maybe he sold—"

"Thank you, Mr. Brown. Now, why did you give him this suit?"

"Well, sir, as I said, he had left Vancouver in a hurry and the weather on this side of the mountains was a good deal colder... And a suit would help him get jobs, and I think what maybe happened was—"

"Just answer the questions please, Mr. Brown. Now, he had left his job and his baby, had left Vancouver with only the clothes he was wearing..." Foss's head pokes forward. "Just one last question, Mr. Brown. After his visit, you and Mrs. Brown gave him a suit and waved him off at the Calgary train station. How much time went by before you saw your nephew again?"

Uncle Art looks across at Rodger, then out into the courtroom. The elderly chin, so much like Rodger's, is set.

"Well, Mr. Brown?"

There is silence. Behind Rodger, in the body of the courtroom, two hundred people breathe as one. It sounds like the panting of a giant animal, the beast *Curiosity*.

"You have to answer the question, Mr. Brown," the judge says gently. Uncle Art looks up at him.

"I do?"

"I'm afraid so, sir."

Uncle Art looks down at his knuckles, lying uselessly on the witness box railing.

"Well, it was a long time." His voice is low, hoarse, an old voice shaky with emotion.

"How long? Five years? Ten? Twenty years?"

There is a pause. The beast holds its breath.

"About ten I guess."

"Isn't that rather a long time, for someone who loved you so well?" Foss asks gently. "You must have wondered about him."

"Yes," Uncle Art glances across at his nephew, tries to smile, "and we prayed for him."

"Thank you, Mr. Brown," Foss smiles, "that will be all."

Cosselli stands up.

Rodger looks down at his hands. Leave the old man alone, he'd like to shout at them, let him go home! Arthur looks so tired, the coat hanger shoulders are struggling to stay squared.

"Mr. Brown," it is Cosselli's turn to smile, "since Mr. Foss appears to want to know all about how interested you and your nephew have been in each other, let's complete the picture for him. We'll start at the present and work backwards, shall we?

"Now, during the last few years, let's say the last fifteen years, have you seen much of your nephew and his family?"

"Oh yes, sir," says Uncle Art, brightening. "You see, Margaret did eventually come back to Vancouver. Rodger visited her in England a few times and then, when she was ready, she came back and both boys lived with her."

"Rodger did not live with her?"

"Well, sir, he did for a while. She had divorced him in England, so when she came back they married all over again... But I guess it was not a marriage made in heaven. They have always remained friends, though. And they both still come down to see us now and then." Uncle Art sends a small smile in Rodger's direction.

"I see," Cosselli nods. "So let me just recap here. The accused made a marriage in the forties during the war and this marriage, like so many of our generation's, had its rocky points. So much so that they divorced. The bond was strong enough, though, that he persevered, kept travelling all the way to England to visit her, and she finally came back and married him over again. It didn't work, but even now, after all these years, the bond between them remains. They are friends."

"That's right, sir," Uncle Art nods vigorously. "Except for that one break—"

"Right. She took off across Canada and he dropped everything to follow her... That must have been quite a relationship. Let's take a look at that relationship—"

"Objection, My Lord," says Foss, half rising. "What earthly relevance, beyond the fact that he was following her, can the nature of the accused's marriage have to this murder trial? It has been established that the accused was not with his wife when he took his fateful trip east in 1947."

"My Lord, I submit that it is of the utmost relevance," Cosselli replies. "The Crown has striven to make a connection between the accused's character, his trip east after the war, and the shooting of a taxi driver in northern Ontario. But it has also been established that the accused was following his wife at the time. Therefore, the defense wishes to explore the accused's frame of mind during this trip. Examining the nature of his marriage will help to do that."

Mr. Justice Harley nods. "The objection is overruled. You may proceed, Mr. Cosselli."

Cosselli bows slightly.

"Thank you, My Lord. Now, Mr. Brown, you have stated that the war experience had an effect upon your nephew, that his wounds rendered him 'weak as a kitten' at first. Did the experience change him in any other way?"

Uncle Art thinks for a minute, then looks across at his nephew.

"Well, yes, to tell you the truth, I think it did. He had been to a lot of places, you see, and he had seen a lot. He had also endured a lot of pain... For a long time after he came back, even after he got strong again, he couldn't seem to settle down... It was as if part of him always wanted to be someplace else... only he himself didn't know where..."

Rodger remembers his excitement on arriving back in England from Sicily and finding a message from Margaret, saying she would visit the next day. He even remembers the date: October 30, 1943. After breakfast the next morning he borrowed the nurse's pocket mirror.

"Have to get all dolled up," he joked, "I've got a lady coming."

But the gaunt, bony face that looked back at him was years older than his own. Dull brown springs of hair lay flat against his head. The eyes in the mirror were empty of hope.

This was not the man Margaret had married. This wizened body that could not even defecate properly, how could he have thought for one moment that she would want him back?

He stared a moment longer, then dropped the mirror onto the blanket, closed his eyes...

"Rodger? Rodger darling."

Oh, no! She was here. Or had he been dreaming? He opened his eyes, saw her standing by his bed, so trim and healthy-looking in her blue WRN's uniform. So beautiful. She was smiling, but her grey eyes looked apprehensive, he thought. He closed his eyes again.

"Rodger, it's me, darling. Maggie."

He kept his eyes shut.

"Please wake up." He heard the tremor in her voice.

He had planned to make a little joke about himself and the fact that it was Hallowe'en, but now that she was actually here: the moment he had waited so long for, had dreamt of, he could not face her. He turned his head away, felt a wetness spread across the pillowcase.

"He's bound to be a little off, Mrs. Brown," explained the nurse's voice. "He can't take much excitement just yet, I'm afraid. You come back tomorrow and I think you'll find him perkier."

"But how is he, nurse?"

"Well he's still weak, but..." Their voices moved away, became a murmur. Now Margaret would be hearing all about the hole in his stomach, the odious colostomy.

She came every evening after that, bringing with her the salty clean smell of England's South Downs, and after a while he would prop himself up against his pillows to play cribbage or gin rummy on a white wooden patient's tray that stood on legs over his body.

Later he was let out for walks, then even for excursions with Margaret into town. He had to promise not to eat— all his meals were given to him intravenously— but he could drink. So they would go out and for the first time in months he felt the breezes on his skin. When the jangles of traffic and people got too much, they would go into a seafront tea shop. The wonderful sweet tastes of orange crush or black currant cordial on his tongue after so long, would fill him with joy, so that he would open right up, telling her about his discovery of books, reciting some of the Robert Service poems. She would smile, relieved, but he could see she was not captured by the poems' spell.

And then suddenly, for no apparent reason— usually it was an oozing in the colostomy dressing, a putrid smell rising, reminding him again that he was not whole, that he could never again be the man who had claimed her, who had promised never to make her sorry— he would destroy the outing by snapping at her.

"Are you feeling tired, darling?" she would reply, concerned.

He would think he'd seen pity, would wrench his arm away.

"I'd better go back now."

Back in bed, his lips would move silently:

There's a land where the mountains are nameless.
And the rivers all run God knows where;
There are lives that are erring and aimless—

"Rodger?" She would lean down to him.

And deaths that just hang by a hair;
There are hardships that nobody reckons;

"Rodger, look at me!"

There are valleys unpeopled and still;
There's a land— oh, it beckons and beckons,
And I want to go back— and I will.

Until her footsteps receded down the corridor.

Then one day in early December Rodger received good news. A hospital ship would take him to Canada the next week. Margaret could follow him two weeks later. They would be home in time for Christmas. He waited for her in the hospital sunroom. Outside, an English sparrow was hopping about on the bare branches of a tree, twittering in the weak morning sunshine. The uniform Rodger was wearing was too large for him now, but freed from the tubes and intravenous bottle for a while, he felt good, healthy, full of new hope. Margaret would meet his family...

The quick tap-tapping of her footsteps sounded down the hall behind him. Turning in his chair, he saw her first. Her face was white against its freckles. Dark shadows stained the skin below her eyes. Had she caught a cold? He felt a sudden surge of warmth, wanted to hug her, to shield her from every possible pain so that those wonderful grey eyes would light with happiness again. She found him, smiled weakly.

"What is it, sweetheart?" She sat down on the sofa next to him. He took her hand. "You look terrible."

She looked down, fiddled with the fastening to her handbag, glanced at him, then down again.

Told him she could not be his wife any more.

New hope, so delicate, shattered easily.

"Why not?" He managed at last. But how could he be surprised?

"Well, I've been thinking and thinking. I've never gone away before, never been anywhere at all, let alone as far away as Canada. And if I am your wife I shall have to come home with you... And there I'd be, all alone on the other side of the world, not knowing a single soul except you and you... you are—" Her chin wobbled. She fumbled in her handbag for a handkerchief.

Rodger could not speak: You are a rag doll of a man, no good to me—

"— You don't seem to want me at all any more."

"Oh no, honey, no! It's not that!"

"What, then?" She looked at him, blinking through her tears. "Why are you so dreadful all the time? I love you, you know that, and you... well, you used to say—"

"I love you too, Margaret. I do!" He tried to draw her towards him but it was hard, she was so much bulkier than he was now, and his arm was so weak, "I... It's just that... I don't know..."

She pulled away, looked at him in shock.

"You mean you don't think I should come with you either?"

Even streaked with tears, her face looked so beautiful. Too beautiful. Anger, resentment welled up inside him. With an effort he pushed it aside. His voice, when he finally spoke, was low.

"I do love you, Margaret, more than you can possibly know, but now I... Well, for Christ's sake, just look at me! How can I take care of you like this? I can't even go to the bathroom, for God's sake... Maybe I never will."

"But Rodger, I don't—"

"No, you don't understand, Margaret! You haven't seen the scars, or the putrid dressings. You don't know the half of it!" He heard his own voice trembling now. He glanced away, his eyes blurring. When finally he could look back, she was smiling.

"No, Rodger, it's you who doesn't understand," she started to laugh and cry all at once. "You are a great vain lumbering idiot."

"What?"

"You never were Clark Gable, you know. And if the putrid dressings are what's worrying you, you can change them yourself. I shall have nothing to do with them. Anyway, Doctor says they'll be able to rebuild your insides so you won't have the dressings any more."

He searched her face. Was she kidding, trying to be brave? But her eyes held no reflection of his doubts, no fear, or repugnance, or pity...

"So Margaret stuck by him through all the pain, his fear. How did she make out over here?" Cosselli is asking.

"She was very much in love with Rodger," Uncle Art answers. "There was no doubt about that, but she was homesick, too. She was in a kind of limbo, don't you see? She had left everything she knew to make a home with Rodger in Vancouver, but he wasn't able to give her much at all at first. There was the time in the hospital, when she had only his mother and little sister for company. Then, when he was recovering, for a long time he could hardly even get out of his chair...

"I remember his first solid meal, after they rebuilt his stomach and got rid of the colostomy. A boiled egg it was. Well, he was in excruciating agony for hours after that... And I think all that was very hard on Margaret. But Bea kept her busy making biscuits, chatting, and I took her out riding with me in the mornings and after a month or so Rodger began to regain some strength..."

Rodger's first day out with her was late in May. The breeze still carried the smell of snow down from the Rockies. Yellow buffalo beans shivered in it, bright, new-green aspen disks danced on it. He and Margaret rode past groups of cattle grazing in the grasses or wading knee-deep in the sloughs, bovine families on a spring picnic.

They stopped for lunch among the yellow clover and the dainty shepherd's purse along the western fence and as they lay snoozing on the picnic blanket after the meal, Rodger heard the clear, bell-like song of a meadowlark. It brought him his youth: freedom, energy, so much hope!

He raised his head to look for it, saw a sudden mischievous puff of breeze sneak between the buttons of Margaret's blouse, caress her breasts, then drop the fabric back into place while still she dozed. The air's chill left her nipples raised.

Rodger turned on his side. He would touch her, that's all. But as he cupped her breast, her eyes opened, found his. He smiled, came closer and the smells of the grass and the horses and the sun mixed with her own sweet body scent. Oh, how long it had been!

Her fingers ran down his back along the spine, then around, under his t-shirt to cover the scars as if they were not there, and then his body was pressed against hers, his hands finding her skin, and then they were both naked out there on the empty range, moving together under the gazes of their horses, into a swirling vortex, towards the fountainhead...

"So in conclusion, Mr. Brown, could we say that this man who was rushing harem-scarem across the country in refrigerator cars had one thing paramount in his mind: to find and bring back his wife?"

"I would say so, yes. He loved his wife, Mr. Cosselli, and he wanted, more than anything, to do right by her and his boys."

Cosselli smiles. "Thank you, sir."

Foss rises to his feet.

"Mr. Brown, you have stated that when your nephew returned from the war he had changed. He was weak, couldn't seem to settle down. He left his pregnant wife to go off to sea. Then, when he went east in '47, he dropped everything— his apprenticeship, even his newborn son— without a second thought. Would it be fair to conclude from that that he was still restless— in terms of his responsibilities— when he travelled east?"

Cosselli's cross-examination has buoyed up the old boy. Art lifts his chin, looks the Crown attorney straight in the eye.

"I do not know about that, sir. All I will attest to is that his wife Margaret and his sons mattered more to him then than anything else in the world."

Rodger smiles at his uncle. But Foss is right too...

They returned to Vancouver from that blissful time at Uncle Art and Aunt Bea's ranch to find that Margaret was pregnant. Rodger's father's shipyard took him on as a boiler room apprentice and they were so full of hope... But within months the shipyard work began to pall. How could he, who had travelled across Europe, seen the world, lived with war, how could he now do the same job day after day, year in, year out, in the place where he had always lived?

Rodger began to take long walks after dinner, leaving Margaret alone while he tramped through neighbourhoods that had not changed at all, even though millions of people— the little girl, his best friend Charlie— had died. He had lost most of his stomach, he was lucky to have survived, but for what?

Then suddenly, when Baby Charlie was just one, Margaret's father died in a car crash. She cried for so long. Rodger would come home and find her eyes dry, but still red, and though she said nothing after the first weeks, tried to carry on, he could see her pain.

He took her and the baby out to walk down by the harbour, or in Stanley Park, and one time Little Charlie, stumbling across the sand after a seagull, lost his balance and fell flat on his face. The bird screeched away and, flapping its huge wings, took flight. Rodger scooped up his son, laughing, but his eyes stayed with the gull as it sailed out across the harbour to sea. Turning finally, he found Margaret watching him. She knew what he was feeling...

When the shipyard offered him a month's stint on a ship bound for Panama, he jumped at the opportunity. Two months after his return, he was offered a three-month voyage to the far east. He was to leave the next morning.

Little Charlie, who was eighteen months old, was staggering around the kitchen floor, playing with the saucepans, when Rodger told Margaret.

"Three months!" Margaret's hand went to her belly, swollen again with six months of pregnancy. He kissed her.

"I can't say no, honey, it's in the blood. And just think how much more money I'll bring home. We'll be able to get a bigger place." He put his hand on her belly, "Don't worry, I'll be back in time."

Charlie dropped a saucepan lid onto his toe, started to shriek. There was no further discussion.

A typhoon off the coast of Japan, followed by mechanical difficulties, stretched three months into six. When finally he bounded up the steps of their brownstone on a wet morning at the end of March, 1947, a bunch of fresh-bought roses in his hand, he found the apartment empty:

I have taken Charlie and gone home to England,
to Mother, leaving you a second son who bears your name.
Perhaps he will matter to you in a way I obviously
cannot. Your mother has him. I love you, Rodger,
and heaven knows I have tried, but without you
there is nothing for me here.

He read the note again, uncomprehending at first. Then anger, a huge anger, larger than he had ever known, took hold of him.

How dare she! She had left him, and taken Little Charlie! He threw down the roses. She had promised to love him! She did love him. So why couldn't she have waited at least, to talk?

Maybe she hasn't really gone, said his hope. Maybe this was all a ruse. The furniture was still here, and the mantel clock her parents had given them for their wedding. Maybe she was just out, staying with one of her friends to teach him a lesson. He ran into the bedroom, tripped over Charlie's little ride'em fire engine, threw open the armoire. Her side was empty. So she had gone. Taken his son, left her new baby, and gone! How could she? What kind of woman would leave her newborn baby! Would take his son away from his father! He drove his fist through the armoire door.

Pain slashed across his knuckles. He looked down. They were bleeding. A splinter stuck out of the skin. He blinked, trying to see it well enough to extract the sliver, realized he was crying.

He went back to the living room, to her note, the only thing left of her, sat with it on the sofa, his raincoat soaking the yellow slipcovers Margaret had made and there was no sound in the apartment. Even the mantel clock had stopped. He sat there a long time, not seeing the room or the roses drooping on the floor where he had thrown them, but seeing her in the kitchen in her apron when he came home, smiling at him, lifting Charlie out of his crib, feeding him, cleaning him up...

Her round schoolgirl's handwriting blurred again as he read and re-read her note. She was so wrong, she did matter to him. And Little Charlie, too.

He went to his parents' house, saw Baby Rodger.

"Just as well, if you ask me," said his mother. "I knew she wasn't a stayer the minute I saw her."

He glared at her, kissed the tiny rumpled cheek of his newborn son.

"Take good care of him for me, Ma. His mother will be back soon."

The next day he started on his way east.

"I have no more questions of this witness," says Foss. He turns to the judge. "My Lord, the Crown's case now moves to the accused's recent statements to police. I believe Mr. Cosselli will ask for a *voir dire?*"

"That is correct, My Lord," Cosselli straightens his papers. "The defense is of the opinion that a *voir dire* at this time is crucial to the carriage of justice in this case."

"Well it is nearly lunch time," says the judge. "Court will adjourn until 2 p.m., and the jury will remain in the jury room until further notice."

"All rise!"

ᨏ CHAPTER 6 ᨎ

In order to rule on its admissibility as evidence, the judge has to hear the testimony at issue in a *voir dire*. I can't publish any of it today, but if the judge rules it admissible, I will hear it all again in open court. If he rules against the testimony, the charge against Rodger will be dismissed and I will be free to put the story into tomorrow's *Chronicle-Journal*.

I watch R.C.M.P. Constable Raymond Kilgore lumber up, through the gate in the railing, to the witness stand. Too many hamburgers on the night shift have given the skin of his face a leathery thickness. He is a stocky man whose muscles, now that he has reached his mid-thirties, are beginning to lose their shape under his tight grey suit. Rodger met him six months ago in a Vancouver bar.

What on earth could have possessed Rodger, I wonder, to choose such a man for a confessor?

"The accused said he had shot a cab driver, back in the forties," Kilgore tells the court.

I can see Rodger wince. Surely he had not been so blunt?

"Would you tell us, please, where and why this conversation took place, Constable?" says Foss.

"Yes, sir. Upon receipt of a call at approximately 1 p.m., Constable Flowers and myself proceeded to the Picadilly Hotel in downtown Vancouver. We found the accused sitting by himself at a table in the bar..."

Rodger had to call twice before anyone showed up. He had
spent all morning getting up his nerve to finally straighten it all out,
and then nobody came. He was on the point of leaving— a man can
only wait so long to voluntarily hang himself— when two large men
in short hair and grey suits appeared in the doorway. Three old
rummies slumped in chairs by the side wall nudged each other,
whispering, as Rodger came to his feet.

"Mr. Jones?" Kilgore asked.

Rodger ran his hands down the side of his pants, took a breath,
nodded. Kilgore eyed Rodger's rumpled windbreaker and pants,
then he and Constable Flowers sat down at the table. It jiggled,
spilling Rodger's beer. Rodger watched the backwash spread a stain
along the undersleeve of Kilgore's jacket, but the man was not the
type who would notice.

"Now, what's this about a confession?" Kilgore looked around
in disdain.

"Well, there... I..." But where to start, how to say it finally, after
all the years? And why bother? They obviously thought he was a
kook... He could smile. But then he thought of Elsa, waiting for
him at home; waiting, as long as he went through with it. He held
onto his glass, "...There was a murder a long time ago—"

"What murder?"

"It was a cab driver in northern Ontario... After the war and
I..." He took momentary refuge in a sip of beer, "I want to tell you
about it."

"Why?"

"Why what?" Rodger's voice went up. Kilgore's questions were
so loud, too fast, bullets punching holes in what little courage he
had mustered. This was not the way it was supposed to go.

"Why tell us about it?"

Rodger stared. Kilgore's heavy face looked impregnable, bored. The younger constable was expressionless. Rodger had expected they would be fully dressed Mounties with red coats, high boots, clear, interested faces.

They had expected a crank, a liquored up old fool! He pushed his glass away and leaned forward.

"No listen, there was a murder in Geraldton, Ontario, back in the forties. A man called Boucher." He stopped. It was the first time he had ever spoken the name.

"So?"

"So I was there."

They said nothing, just sat there like a couple of grey lumps.

"There were no trains from Geraldton," he told them, "that's why we... had to get a cab, and there was this gun, and..." His whole body was trembling. He tried to lift his glass, but the beer slopped over the rim. He put it down again, tried to go on, but twenty-five years of silence welled up inside his chest.

"And?" Kilgore blinked like a lizard.

"And... well," he cried finally, "I think... maybe I shot him."

Over by the wall the rummies peered out of the shadows like mice...

Foss is nodding pensively. "What was the accused's demeanour during the conversation in the bar, Constable?"

"He was upset— his face was red and there were tears in his eyes when he spoke about the murder— but he was completely rational."

"And what did you do after this conversation?"

"We asked him to come down to the station to make a written statement."

"And did he come?"

"Yes, sir. He was very willing to co-operate."

Rodger has told me about the police station interview room: a scuffed desk with a couple of straightbacked chairs in front of it, white tile walls and a girly calendar advertising a local bathroom tile company.

"I telexed Thunder Bay," Kilgore continues. "When word came back that a taxi driver called Boucher had been killed in 1947, and the case was still unsolved, we cautioned Mr. Jones and took a statement from him."

"Would you read that statement to us now, please, Constable?" Foss hands him the document.

Kilgore begins to read, "Around 1946 or '47 I was hitching freight trains in Ontario and Manitoba and there was quite a party going on... We got off somewhere around northern Ontario and took a cab to go to Hearst."

Behind Rodger the beast *Curiosity* is still, the air in the court-room completely silent. Kilgore's voice is devoid of expression.

"Somewhere along the road we pulled out a gun. We told the driver to stop and then we shot him."

Shot him. The beast gobbles up the words. Rodger closes his eyes.

"The driver didn't have a chance," Kilgore continues. "I hauled him out of the cab and left him in the snowbank. There was blood all over the place. I threw the gun over the snowbank. Then we drove the cab to Hearst and I got a train to Ottawa. My pants had blood on them so I threw them off the train."

The pants? I look up. The blood on the pants was not Boucher's, we have established that.

"Do you want the questions, too?" Kilgore asks.

"Please."

"I asked: 'You said *we shot him*. Who is *we?*'"

"Jones said: 'There were two French Canadians.'

"'Who actually shot the driver?'

"'I did.'"

I look at Rodger. Did he really say that, right out? Why, if he does not know, did he say that?

Maybe he did shoot Boucher, I realize suddenly. The thought is a shock. It sheds a new, cold blue light on my thinking.

Could it be that far from being naive, this prisoner is very, very clever? I remember Cosselli's accusing him of holding something back... What if he did shoot Boucher and knows it, so that his confession is real? My heart sinks. Could it be that I am the one who is hopelessly naive? I like the man. I have sat up nights talking to him, have bared my soul to him. Have sacrificed my reporter's objectivity to him...

Is that what Cosselli has wanted to happen? Is that why he has given me such unheard-of access to his client?

Is this whole trial, and my story, a con?

I begin to shiver. Because what we have here is: one, a lawyer whose brain is smooth as greased lightning; two, a shifty, clever, fifty-six-year-old man; and three, me: a twenty-three-year-old cub reporter. Which one of us is most likely to have been fooled? And whom but the one holding the pen, telling the world, is it most advantageous to dupe?

No wonder Cosselli encouraged me to get close to Rodger Brown...

Kilgore is continuing. "'Why did you do it?'

"'I don't know, it was stupidity.'

"'Where did you get the gun?'

"'I bought it from somebody in Winnipeg, I don't remember his name.'

"'What kind of gun was it?'

"'I don't know. It was large, had a kick on it like a mule.'"

How could you know that, asshole, unless you fired it?

"'Can you describe the driver?'

"'He was younger than I was... that's all I remember.'

"'How did you know his name?'

"'When I woke up in Ottawa I read in the paper that Raymond Boucher was killed in Geraldton and I realized that this was the cab driver we... killed.'

"'Did this Boucher provoke you in any way?'

"'No.'

"'Were you ever approached by the police regarding this murder?'

"'Yes, about the pants I threw off the train. I lied and nothing was done about it.'

"'Describe the pants.'

"'They were part of a two-pants suit. I think they were brown.'

"'Why have you contacted police now?'

"'It's my girlfriend. She knows there is something on my mind.'" Kilgore looks at the Crown attorney.

Foss nods, mulling over what he has heard, then he hooks his fingers into his waistcoat watchpockets. His gown flares out from his elbows, his crow stance.

"Constable, did you know at the time you took that statement that the name of the man you were interviewing was not Jones?"

"No, sir."

"But the man who sits before this court today is the man who talked to you in the bar, who gave you the written statement and who signed himself Jones?"

"Yes, sir."

"How did your Mr. Jones behave during and after this statement?"

"Well, he was nervous, chain-smoking, but he was eager to help. You could see it was a great relief to him to confess."

Was that it then, Rodger, I wonder? Was it relief, having the steamroller of guilt lifted off your chest, that brought you here?... But if that is so, why haven't you pleaded guilty?

"How could you see his relief?" Foss asks.

"Well, he seemed to calm down once it was out. He even made a joke."

Over at the lawyers' table Cosselli is scribbling notes.

"Constable," Foss continues, "you and Constable Flowers were the only ones with Mr. Jones during all this time. Did either of you offer him anything prior to his making the statement?"

"Only a cup of coffee, cigarettes."

"Now please think carefully. Did you say anything to him that could be considered a threat or an inducement of any kind?"

"No, sir, I did not."

Foss smiles, a schoolmaster whose student is performing well.

"Constable, how long have you been an R.C.M.P. officer?"

"Fifteen years, sir."

"And are you convinced that this statement was taken properly according to the law?"

"Yes, sir."

"Thank you, Constable, that will be all."

Kilgore continues to stand, solid as a rock, in the witness box: a federal officer of the law with no stake in this except to tell the truth, the whole truth, and nothing but the truth.

Cosselli takes his time coming to his feet, adjusts his bi-focals to take a last glance at his notes, then takes them off, leaves the table. He likes to use the space between it and the bench, to move back and forth, raise his arms, pace like a caged lion— whatever suits the nature of his questioning.

"Constable Kilgore, I noticed that during your testimony about the conversation in the bar you did not refer to written notes. Yet this conversation took place six months ago. Did you not record the statement in the bar?"

"No, sir. I made notes later of the incident in the bar, but I did not consider it necessary at the time to record our actual conversation with Mr. Jones."

"Why not?"

"I wanted to do some investigation first to see whether there had in fact been a taxi driver murdered in northern Ontario in 1947."

Cosselli nods, understanding.

"You wanted to find out, in other words, whether this was just another drunken crank. Now, Constable, you stated that when you were in the bar with the accused he appeared upset. Would you tell us again, how exactly did you discern that he was upset?"

"Well, there was the crying, and his face was red, and he was fidgeting."

"Had he been drinking?"

"...There was a glass of beer in front of him but it was full. He was not impaired."

"Did he smell of beer, Constable?"

Kilgore hesitates.

"Well?"

"Sir, even a mouthful of beer smells—"

"So he drank beer while you were there?"

Kilgore pauses. Rodger watches, his jaw set.

"He had a sip or two, yes."

"So he smelled of beer."

"The whole place smelled of beer, including him."

"Fine. So he was drinking beer and he was red in the face and crying. Were there any other signs of intoxication?"

"Objection!" Foss is hot. "The constable has not attributed the signs to intoxication."

"Sustained." Mr. Justice Harley looks reprovingly at Cosselli.

"I beg the court's pardon, My Lord." Cosselli walks over to stand directly facing the witness. "I can easily deal with this another way. Constable, you have had experience with people who are impaired. Are not glassy eyes, slurred speech, unsteadiness usually signs of impairment?"

"They can be."

"Is a flushed face a sign of impairment?"

"Sometimes."

"And uncontrolled emotion such as shouting or crying?"

"Sometimes." Kilgore cranks his chin higher.

"And he smelled of beer. He had a glass of beer in front of him. Did you ask him how many others he had drunk?"

"No, sir. He was not impaired."

"Having decided to take him in for questioning about a murder, did you ask him to submit to a breathalyser test, or make any inquiries at the bar about the extent of his drinking?"

"No, sir, I saw no need. In my judgement the man was not impaired."

"He was flushed, he cried, he was drinking beer, but you decided, having no idea how much he had drunk, that he was not impaired." Cosselli gazes at the constable.

"Now, you asked him to come to the police station. Was he charged with anything?"

"No, sir, not yet."

"Why not?"

"I did not yet know whether there had even been a murder."

"Ah... And if he had refused to come? Would you have arrested him then?"

Kilgore thinks about this, decides to nod.

"Yes, sir, I believe I would have... I thought there might be something to his confession—"

"So, technically he was under arrest."

Cosselli is moving so fast. He is so powerful, so much in control. I have no choice but to wonder: was Rodger impaired that day? He said he had had a few beers while he was waiting, but how many? Did they have any effect on what he said? Kilgore, meanwhile, is not answering the question.

"Well, Constable, was he under arrest or wasn't he?"

"I guess you could say he was," Kilgore says grudgingly.

"So he was under arrest. You did not judge it necessary to record his statement in the bar, or to find out how many beers he had drunk, but you did judge it necessary to arrest him." Cosselli leaves a pause. Kilgore shifts uncomfortably in the witness box.

"Now, you took the accused to the station. How long was it then before you sent your telex?"

"Maybe twenty minutes. We chatted with the accused for a little while first. As I said, he was very upset."

"You chatted for a while. You have notes about this chat?"

"No, sir, I do not."

"So you are telling this court that you will arrest a man without confirmation that there has even been a murder, but then you will not take notes for the benefit of the accused at his trial?" Cosselli's black eyes bore into the witness.

"It was just a casual conversation—"

"Constable, when you arrest a man, it is not you who decides when a conversation with him is germane. Have you not learned that in fifteen years?" Kilgore's leathery face colours.

108

"I believe my partner made some notes," he says lamely.

But Cosselli has already turned away. When he speaks again he is back at his seat behind the table, his bi-focals perched on the end of his nose. All the tone has been removed from his voice, leaving only disdain.

"The accused's statement says: 'Around 1946 or '47 I was hitching freights... I got off somewhere around northern Ontario...'" Cosselli looks over the top of his glasses at Kilgore, "Mr. Jones' facts are very vague in places, aren't they?"

"His memory of details was not all that clear," Kilgore admits.

"An event had been bothering him for twenty-five years, enough to make him finally come to the police, but he remembered no details..." Cosselli refers back to his notes. "Half the time he says 'we,' half the time 'I.' Didn't that strike you as odd, Constable?"

"Not really, sir. There could have been many reasons for his vagueness." But the stuffing has gone out of Kilgore.

"After you took the statement, what did you do?"

"We searched him, then locked him in a cell."

"What did you find when you searched him?... You were making notes by now, I take it?"

"Yes, sir," Kilgore produces a small police-issue notepad. "A pencil, handkerchief and two dollars were found."

"No identification?"

"No, sir."

Cosselli starts to ask another question, thinks better of it, and changes course.

"You locked him up, why? Had you charged him with anything?"

"No, but we were holding him on suspicion of the Boucher murder until Inspector Richardson of the Ontario Provincial Police arrived."

"I see... on suspicion." Cosselli waves a hand, indicating that he is finished.

I frown. Maybe I am wrong, nobody is putting anything over on me... Maybe. But still I hope Rodger can feel the beast's breath hot on his neck.

⟮ CHAPTER 7 ⟯

"Detective Inspector Allan Richardson!"

Last night Rodger told me that Kilgore and Flowers had left him in a cell for two whole days without even a razor to shave with. He had gone nearly crazy: they couldn't just leave him there, could they? Surely you got a trial, even if you confessed? But nobody had come near him, nobody he could ask anything, anyway.

Then finally, on the third day, Richardson appeared, a tall, dark-haired, serious man in a well-cut blue suit who shook hands firmly, as if Rodger were a person worth knowing.

"I'm from the Ontario Provincial Police's Criminal Investigation Branch, Rodger," he smiled. "I'm here to help you get this thing cleared up. That's what you want, isn't it?"

Relief, oh blessed relief, it washed over him, Rodger told me. It felt so good to get everything out into words, to talk to the inspector about the doubt, the nightmares, the questions that had been chewing away like rats at his brain all these years...

Now I sit in court remembering the way his brown eyes had held mine while he told me, the way his mobile face had creased and uncreased into a variety of expressions during the telling of the story, and I wonder how much of it is true.

He says he has come here looking for the truth. But if he does not know what that is, why would he damn himself by telling the police he did shoot the man? Unless he did shoot Boucher, and is now playing a game in which the stakes are the relief of confession coupled with the return of his freedom.

I glance across the courtroom to the prisoner's box. Rodger looks relaxed. He is smiling at the inspector.

The inspector must be concentrating on what he is about to say, however, because he does not appear to notice.

"Inspector Richardson, how long have you served with the Ontario Provincial Police?" Foss begins.

"Eighteen years, sir." Allan Richardson feels at home in the courtroom. It is the gift of experience— both his own and his father's— say those who have watched him. But there is more to it than that. The truth is that Richardson loves the courtroom, loves the challenge of pitting his intelligence and his policeman's skills against defense counsels' mental and oratorical gymnastics.

"The trial is the end point upon which all the strategies I have used in my investigations are focused: the pay-off," he told me in an interview on his way in from the airport this morning. "You can be as sure as grass is green that you have the right man— a smart cop wouldn't book him unless he was— but there are always weaknesses in your case. You shore them up every way you know how, but still, one wrong move anywhere down the line, one ill-considered answer in the course of cross-examination, and a smart lawyer will slip your man out through your fingers.

"Do it right, though, and no legal loophole in the land can save your man."

"When you received a telephone call from the R.C.M.P. in Vancouver about this Jones, you resurrected the file on the Boucher murder," Foss stands beside the table, checking his notes. "Did you recognize any names in that file?"

"The name of my father, Gordon Richardson. He was also an O.P.P. inspector, and as it happened, was the officer in charge of the original murder investigation."

"Is your father still alive, Inspector?"

The question is necessary— Richardson knows Foss must seal off any opportunity for the defense to write him off as his father's avenger— but still Richardson's back stiffens.

"Yes, sir, he is eighty-three."

"And when you saw his name in the file, how did you feel? Did it add to your interest in solving the case?"

Richardson keeps his face expressionless.

"Certainly I have been very interested in solving this unusual case, Mr. Foss. Like my father before me, I am anxious to see justice done— but only by bringing in the right man."

"Have you discussed the case with your father, Inspector?"

"I am afraid a recent stroke has left my father with very little memory."

Sometimes, though, the clouds part for a few minutes, long enough for him to tell a long, rambling story in which every detail is crystal clear. So Richardson has tried again and again, going to the nursing home, holding his father's hand and repeating the names: Boucher, Geraldton, Brown. But the old man's milky eyes just smile vacantly back.

"I'm sorry to hear that, Inspector," says Foss. "Now, perhaps you will tell us when you first met the accused?"

"I met him on May 1, 1972. Constable Flowers brought him into an interview room at the Vancouver detachment of the R.C.M.P. I introduced myself and asked him his name and address. He told me 'Rodger Jones' and gave no address."

"He was a bedraggled-looking individual at first glance, your typical stubble-chinned rubby— except for the eyes. They were not crafty, like so many of the old geezers', but curiously boyish, without guile.

"I informed him that I was going to take him to Thunder Bay where he would be charged with non-capital murder, but first I was going to take another statement from him. I then read him the Ontario police caution—"

"Just a moment, Inspector. Have you told us everything that was said to the accused by everyone in the room, prior to the taking of this statement?"

"Yes, sir. I was the only one who spoke to him."

"And the man you were speaking to as Rodger Jones is the man who now stands before this court?"

"Definitely."

"Did you know at that time that Jones was not his real name?"

"No, sir, I did not."

"Now, Inspector, the accused had been incarcerated for two days. What was his state of mind when you met him?"

"He was sober and alert. He appeared to be at ease."

Foss nods, rocking forward.

"Please, carry on with the cautions, Inspector."

Richardson looks down at his notepad.

"I said: 'Do you wish to say anything in answer to the charge? You are not obliged to say anything unless you wish to do so, but whatever you say may be given in evidence at your trial.'" Richardson glances up. "Then I also said: 'If you have spoken to any police officer or anyone in authority or if any such person has spoken to you in connection with this case, I want it clearly understood that I do not want it to influence you in making any statement. Do you understand what I have just said to you?' Jones replied: 'Oh yeah.'"

"Now, Inspector, after you read the two cautions, and before the statement itself was taken, did you or anyone else say anything to the accused?"

"No, sir."

Foss nods.

"Please read the statement, then."

"I said: 'I am investigating the murder of Raymond Boucher of Geraldton, Ontario in April, 1947. What, if anything, do you wish to tell us about it?'

"The accused replied: 'I was travelling east in northern Ontario and there was a lot of boozing going on. I had never met the others before. We got hold of a gun and then someone suggested we get a cab to go to Hearst. Somewhere along the road it happened. I woke up in the Ottawa railyard and I felt so bad. I knew I had done something wrong. Then I read about it in the paper and I knew I had been there. It's been on my mind a long, long time and finally, well, this is the only way I can get it off my chest.'

"Then I said: 'I will ask you some questions to clear up some points in your statement. Do you wish to answer them?' He said: 'Yes.'

"I said: 'You say you *never met the others before*. Who are you referring to?'

"'A couple of fellows I met in a boxcar.'

"'Where was this?'

"'Oh, boy... In Winnipeg.'

"'You said *somewhere along the road it happened*. What happened?'

"'That I shot the driver.'" Richardson looks up. There it is, folks: the man's guilt as clearly stated as the sentence. Richardson shoots a glance a the prisoner's box. Too bad, I can see him thinking, the man is a nice fellow: polite, intelligent, very friendly. But guilty. Why else did he call the police, put himself through all this?

"Constable Flowers had taken down the statement. He read it back to Mr. Jones and asked him if he wished to sign it," finishes Richardson. "'Oh yes,' he said, and did so."

"Inspector," asks Foss, "was there anything at all in the accused's attitude that suggested that he was afraid, nervous, or hesitant at all about making this statement?"

"No, sir, quite the contrary."

Why is Rodger nodding? *I shot the driver*, he told the police. Did he confess so that they would take him seriously?... Or because deep down he knows the real truth?

"Did his attitude change during or after giving the statement?"

"No, sir."

"Inspector, after taking the statement did you have any further conversations with Mr. Brown on the subject of the murder?"

"Yes, sir, I did. During the course of my investigation I had several."

Ah, Rodger nods again, smiling, expectant: now they will get into the meat of it.

"When and where?"

"In Vancouver, on the plane on the way to Thunder Bay, later when we searched the highway for the gun— I spoke to him several times during those days."

"And what was the subject of these conversations?"

"Well, some of them had to do with my investigation, some were just passing the time of day."

Foss smiles.

"Thank you, Inspector, that is all."

All! Rodger sits bolt upright. His hands grip the railing, as if he will spring to his feet: Wait a minute, that's not all! That's not even the half of what we talked about! He glares at Richardson.

The inspector gazes placidly past him into the courtroom.

What is it, I wonder? Surely Rodger realizes that Foss and Richardson are working together, their only aim to put him behind bars? Richardson has long since decided Rodger is guilty.

Now Cosselli is on his feet.

"Inspector, why did you decide, upon your arrival in Vancouver from Toronto, to take a second written statement from the accused? Was it because you were not satisfied with the statement taken by Constable Kilgore?"

"I always make it a point to take my own statement." Richardson stands straight but relaxed, a match for any adversary.

Cosselli nods, understanding.

"A very prudent precaution. The sign of a dedicated police officer, if I may say so, Inspector... It has been established that your father, too, was an O.P.P. inspector in the Criminal Investigation Branch. Was it he who persuaded you to adopt this career?"

"Objection," Foss sounds bored. "That is hardly relevant to this murder case."

"My Lord, may I remind my learned friend that it was the Crown who introduced the witness' father into this case," Cosselli says. "Also, I can assure the court that the relevance of this line of questioning will soon become apparent."

"The sooner the better, Mr. Cosselli," comments the judge. "You may proceed."

"My father never exerted any pressure on me, if that's what you mean," Richardson replies.

"But as a youth, you naturally would have been interested in his work, in the excitement, the adventure of police detective work?"

"...Yes," Richardson is cautious, "as I imagine most boys would be."

"And you admired your father?"

"I respected him. I still do. He has had a very successful career."

Cosselli nods again.

"A career you respected enough to emulate, that you might even like to match. Inspector Richardson," he continues without giving the witness time to comment, "have you ever worked on a case with your father?"

"No, sir. He had retired by the time I came to the Criminal Investigation Branch."

"So this case provided you with rather a unique opportunity—to work alongside your father in effect, to solve his case, maybe even to match him?"

I listen, fascinated. Richardson is so impassive, so tall and correct, so authoritative in his dark blue suit and greying black hair. Not the sort of man you think of as someone's admiring son.

"My father's involvement in this case interested me, of course," Richardson says carefully, "but it had no effect on the nature of my investigation."

"It just increased your desire to solve the case, perhaps?"

"I don't think so," Richardson smiles. "I always have a desire to solve my cases."

Cosselli smiles back.

"And indeed your successes are evidence that you are your father's son..." He pauses, ostensibly to review his notes. "Now, Inspector, let us go back to your study of your father's file. Mr. Brown was interviewed in 1947 and his name appears in that file. You say you did not know, but did you suspect, when you took your written statement from him, that Rodger Jones was in fact the Rodger Pearse Brown mentioned in the 1947 investigation?"

There is a pause.

"...Yes, sir, I believe I did, although he had not yet been questioned about that."

"What precisely led you to suspect this? Was it that Jones was from Vancouver and there had only been one Vancouverite origi-nally investigated? Or was it his reference to the pants?"

"I cannot say for certain. People move back and forth across the country, so geography would not have influenced me to make the connection. To my mind it was nothing specific; call it a policeman's hunch."

"But you did suspect, when you met him and took the written statement, that Jones was in fact Brown?"

"I cannot say for certain exactly when I began to suspect this."

"Isn't it an obvious suspicion? Wouldn't any detective as successful as you are have suspected it, because of the pants if for no other reason? The question is, why did you not confront Mr. Jones with your suspicion? Why did you not ask him if he was really Rodger Pearse Brown?"

"At that time, it was only a hunch. I therefore saw no need to."

"How did you find out for certain that Jones was Brown?"

"He told me so himself."

"Oh? When?"

"During an interview later that same day."

"How much later?"

"About an hour."

Rodger smiles. Now we'll get to it. They had brought him back to the same interview room. He thought it was so he and Richardson could go on working together, trying to get to the bottom of this, to find his memory...

"And is there any record in existence of this interview?"

"Yes, sir. I taped it."

"Oh? How?"

"There was a tape recorder in the drawer of the desk."

"And was Mr. Brown apprised of this?"

"No, sir."

"Why not?"

"Well, sir, as I have said, I was investigating a murder. I was under no obligation, and I saw no reason to tell him."

"Why did you have this conversation taped?"

"There were a few things I wanted to ask him and I wanted a record of the information."

"Why did you not simply ask Flowers to keep writing?"

"It was going to be a question and answer session and the tape recorder is swifter and more efficient for that kind of interview."

"And this interview was a continuation of the written statement an hour earlier."

"There were just some points I wanted to clear up."

"It was a clarification, in other words, of the accused's statement?"

"Yes, I suppose you could say that."

Cosselli hands the court clerk a thick sheaf of paper to enter as evidence.

"Your Lordship, that taped conversation has a direct bearing on this *voir dire*. This is a transcript of it. I ask that the inspector be allowed to read the relevant sections."

Mr. Justice Harley assents and Richardson begins to read. His voice takes Rodger back into the police station interview room.

The girly calendar was gone. He sat in one of the chairs, Flowers in another one behind him, out of the way, while the inspector paced behind the desk. Somebody had given Rodger a cup of coffee and he remembers how he felt so completely at ease because now there were no notebooks, no cautions, just this man who was trying to help him.

"'In your statement, Rodger, you say you were travelling east,' Richardson asked, 'Where were you going?'

"'I was planning to get a ship out of Montreal.'

"'Why?'

"'I had my Canadian Seafarers' Union papers and I had heard the Franconia was hiring out of Montreal. She was waiting for the ice to break.'

"'You said that in northern Ontario you were with two guys you had met. Tell me about them.'

"'Well, I don't remember much. They were French Canadians. I met them in a boxcar. The one was as big as a mountain and they were both drunk as lords on cheap wine, that I do remember.'

"'And the gun was theirs?'

"'Yeah. The gun was theirs.'

"'And you all got a ride with a shoe salesman to Geraldton.'

"'It must have been Geraldton.'

"'Once you were in Geraldton how did you find the cab? Did you go to the taxi stand?'

"'I forget.'

"'You forget. Well, were there two of you or three in the cab?'

"'There were three in the beginning, but I have an idea there were only two in the cab... I don't know. All I know is I was there. I was in the back seat with a jug of wine or maybe there were two jugs of wine.'

"'Can you think back, Rodger?' Richardson urged. 'Was one of the fellows you met wearing a yellow Hudson's Bay coat?'

Rodger could not remember. Nor could he recall ripping off the taxi sign or stopping for gas in Hearst.

"'I really don't think I did,' he said, 'I wish to God I could remember more about it.'

"'How much money did you get from the wallet, Rodger?'

"'Oh, I never got any wallet. I had a few bucks in my pocket.'

"'And you had the gun?'

"'Yes... I had the gun.'

"'Why did you do it, Rodger?'

"'I have no idea,' he had replied sadly, 'No idea at all. There was no provocation... I just can't figure it out at all.'

"'When you got to Hearst was there still somebody with you?'

"'I think there must have been because I was in no shape to drive, I know that. It was snowing and the road was frozen... It must have been pretty risky... I wish I could help you out more...'"

What a sucker he was.

"'Rodger, is your real name Rodger Pearse Brown?'

"'... Yes.'"

He thought he was safe.

"'Why did you change it?'

"'I don't want to hurt my family... My mother is up in years and I really don't want her to get involved.'

"'Rodger, I have a report here made by Constable Lucas in 1947. You told him you met two French Canadians in Winnipeg, sold them your tweed suit for seven dollars... You said you went on east via Nipigon and Toronto. Were you lying then?'

"'Nipigon? Whereabouts is that?'

"'It's in northern Ontario.'

"'Well, then maybe I went that way? It's a long time ago.'

"'Did you sell the suit?'

"'I don't know. I must have... Except if I was wearing them and had sold the others...?'

I begin to see how confused Rodger was when they took the story apart. None of the facts are clear inside the muddled, muffled place that is his memory. The reading of the transcript continues; Richardson has returned to the murdered driver.

"'Did you hit him after you shot him or before?'

"'No, it was just the one shot... Just a shot...'

"'Did you ever tell your wife or anybody anything at all about this?'

"'No, never. I have never mentioned it to a single soul all these years.'

"'And it has bothered you?'

"'Every day. For twenty-five years I've been wracking my brain, feeling so guilty and not knowing why exactly, just knowing there's something there... That's why this... I need to get the whole thing hashed out.'

"'And are you feeling better now? Is it a load off your mind?'

"'Oh, yes.'

"'And you're sure you can't remember anything else?'

"'So help me, I have tried. But all I get is a void... And a big black question mark.'

"'But you do remember that you pulled the trigger?'

"'Well, yes... there was so much blood. I've never been able to get that blood out of my head.'

"'We would like to talk to your mother and your family, Rodger.'

"'No. I'm sorry, you can't. They don't know a thing about this, and whatever happens I don't want them involved.'"

Richardson's voice comes to a halt. Over at the press table I am writing furiously. This *voir dire* is the trial, and here we have the only truths that matter, surely: the gun, the shot, the guilt. No details, but still, if Rodger recalls shooting the taxi driver, what else is relevant?

"Inspector, you now knew that Brown had signed his confession under a false name. Why did you not insist that he sign it again using his proper name?"

"I did not consider it necessary."

"You did not consider it necessary that a man confessing to murder should do so under his own name?"

"There was no doubt that Jones and Brown were one and the same, he was no longer hiding his identity, and that was all that mattered."

"Inspector, you have told us you gave the accused two separate cautions. The second one: 'If anyone has said anything to you about this,' etcetera, etcetera. Why did you take the trouble to do this?"

"I was ensuring the integrity of the statement."

"And isn't the proper name also essential to the integrity of the statement?"

Richardson looks mildly exasperated.

"Sir, I maintain that at the time the statement was taken the accused's identity was not in question. Later he freely admitted to his name. Therefore it has no bearing on the integrity of his statement."

"Well then, after he had admitted his name, why not have him sign it on the statement— since it did not matter one way or the other?"

"I will repeat, I did not consider it at all necessary."

Cosselli's tone hardens.

"And I will submit that it was because after the taped interview you knew for certain that he would refuse. He had made it very clear that he did not want his family involved, and you knew that his refusal to sign his proper name to the confession would jeopardize the quality of the written statement you had taken such pains to secure."

"He gave his name freely," Richardson insists. "I do not believe he would have refused."

Now Cosselli looks puzzled.

"Inspector, didn't the use of an alias and the lack of identification on a man who was willing to give his name freely strike you as odd?"

"Not really, under the circumstances."

"What about the absence of any criminal record and the fact that he was confessing to a twenty-five-year-old murder?"

"The length of time that had elapsed was certainly highly unusual, but not the absence of a record. Many people convicted of murder do not have a criminal record."

"Nevertheless, when you put all these unusual facts together, did it not suggest anything— that the man you were interviewing might be emotionally unstable, for instance— especially in view of his frame of mind when Constable Kilgore met him?"

"No, sir, I did not have that impression at all."

"You drew no conclusions at all about this man?" Cosselli raises his bushy eyebrows, gestures towards Rodger, as if this is hard to believe.

"I did not think him unstable."

"It sounds from the tape as if the man was very eager to help you." Cosselli begins to move around the end of the table. Richardson's eyes follow him.

"He was."

"In fact, it sounds as if the atmosphere was extremely congenial in there."

Richardson shrugs.

"I was just doing my job, Mr. Cosselli."

"Exactly, sir, that is what I mean," Cosselli is facing the witness box now. "You saw it as your job to create a warm atmosphere in that little room. I submit that as an experienced and successful police inspector, you detected immediately the fragile emotional state of this man." Cosselli's voice begins to rise. "You knew he would respond to friendship, so you gave him that: a warm, secure, helping atmosphere in which your suggestions, once planted, would flourish: 'You went to Geraldton?' 'It must have been Geraldton.' 'You had a gun?' 'Yes, I had the gun.'... And so on. Just agree, that's all he had to do, and you would give him help and support in his hour of need!" Cosselli's voice is booming now, filling the courtroom. "You are a skilled interrogator, sir. I submit that you used that skill to obtain the answers that suited your purpose."

"Objection!"

"Sustained."

But there is no need to protect this witness. His professionalism is a suit of armour. He looks coolly at Cosselli and the matter-of-fact voice with which he replies throws defense counsel's rising crescendoes into melodramatic relief.

"Sir, I was not persecuting Mr. Brown, I was simply trying to dig some facts out of a very foggy twenty-five-year-old memory."

"His memory was indeed foggy... In fact, great chunks of it were missing altogether, weren't they? 'Did you go to the taxi stand?' 'I forget.' 'Why did you shoot the man?' 'I have no idea.' 'Was there somebody with you?' He doesn't know. The written statement itself is so vague as to be practically meaningless. But that didn't strike you as odd, Inspector? Wouldn't you have expected a killer to have every detail of his crime indelibly engraved in his mind?"

"Not necessarily. It is my experience that emotion can cause the mind to play all kinds of tricks." One corner of Richardson's mouth twitches up. "As you know, sir."

"That, Inspector, is precisely what we are here to show." Cosselli turns back towards his seat.

"I have no more questions of this witness."

Mr. Justice Harley leans towards the witness.

"Inspector, there was more on that tape than the parts you have just read. To what does the rest of it refer?"

"Oh, I asked Mr. Brown about his work over the years, who his friends were..."

"And this tape recording was a continuation of the written statement?"

"Well, not exactly, Your Lordship... It was just that I wanted more information."

Cosselli is on his feet in the instant.

"Inspector, did you or did you not tell me less than ten minutes ago that the taped interview was a continuation, or clarification of the written statement?"

"Well, sir, questions in it arose from the written statement, yes, but—"

"Just answer 'yes' or 'no' please. Did you tell me just now that the tape session was a clarification of the written statement?"

"Yes."

"Thank you, Inspector."

Foss is already on his feet.

"Inspector Richardson, I will ask you again: when you found out, after taking the written statement, that Rodger Jones was in reality Rodger Brown, were you satisfied that his alias was not an attempt to deceive you?"

"Oh, yes. He was perfectly willing to admit to his real name."

"Now, after you obtained your written statement the accused was taken away. You studied various reports in your file and thought about your investigation, then you had the accused brought back. Inspector, for the sake of absolute clarity I will ask you one final time: was the tape recording part and parcel of the written statement or was it not?"

Richardson knows the answer. His face is set now, all trace of the friendliness Rodger had known are gone from it.

"It was not. It was not a statement at all. It was part of my on-going investigation."

"Thank you, Inspector." Foss turns to the bench. "My Lord, the Crown has no more witnesses to call on the *voir dire*."

"Court will adjourn until ten o'clock tomorrow morning," says Mr. Justice Harley.

"Well, Rodg', their half of the inning is over." Cosselli comes over to lean on the railing around the prisoner's box. He looks pleased with himself. "Tomorrow it'll be our turn at bat."

But Rodger is only half listening.

I shot him. Three times his mother has heard him say it. If only he could see her, tell her the whole thing—

"Can you get hold of my mother, Peter? Tell her to come and see me?"

I am mulling over the case as I struggle to unlock the door to my basement apartment. Inside, the telephone begins to ring. I jiggle the key in the troublesome lock, then finally, three rings later, fling open the door, drop my handbag, lunge across the kitchen towards the receiver. And slam the toes of my right foot into the corner of the kitchen counter.

Pain— crashing cymbals, drum rolls— builds in the ball of my foot. I grit my feet, hop the last step to the telephone. The line is dead.

"Damn! Damn, damn, damn!" I hop on my good foot, waiting for the drumming pain to subside. It was John, I know it was. He often calls just after six, to see what I'm doing, when I'll be coming to Ottawa next. He will have read my stories on this case. The Ottawa papers picked them up, my editor told me this morning.

So, was he phoning to congratulate me, to support my efforts, chew over my doubts with me, help me devise a strategy for tonight's visit with Rodger... to hear what I need, and then provide it? I flop onto a kitchen chair.

Or would my stream of excitement have been greeted by a pause— "Oh"— then a change of subject to airplane arrival schedules and how much he misses me?

I remove my shoes and get up to peel my pantyhose— stupid bloody court clothes— off the injured leg. Why can't I wear boots to court? My toes are safe in boots. I cradle my poor foot. The baby toe is beginning to swell.

You're such a jerk, John. "What does it matter where you work, as long as we're together?" You actually said that! How could you be so selfish?

I have asked him this when we are together, fighting because it is nearly time for me to leave again and neither of us can see any way to change that.

He denies ever having said it.

"Oh? So why don't you quit being a bureaucrat and come out to Thunder Bay, then?" I counter. "I'll tell you why. Because down in your heart of hearts, John, it is you, not us— the working out of your life, not ours— that matters most to you."

He'll phone again.

Well I'll show him. I hop across the kitchen, wrench the cold water tap on to fill the sink, wince as my foot meets the icy water. I won't be here when he calls. I don't need him any more than he needs me. I am independent, am I not?

Now the bite of the cold water is worse than the pain. I withdraw my foot, put it down gingerly on a tea towel on the floor.

Can I walk, I wonder?

❧ CHAPTER 8 ❧

"Br-r-rown! You have a visitor: a Mrs. Brown."

Margaret Brown the younger, Rodger's ex-wife twice over, slipped into the courtroom this afternoon— a middle-aged woman with wavy brown hair shot through with silver, smartly dressed in a navy blue skirt suit. Her startling grey eyes told me who she was. So when court adjourned I introduced myself. She asked me the way to the jail. I offered to meet her at the Prince Arthur Hotel after dinner and drive her. Now I hobble away, to give her some privacy in the prisoners' visiting room.

Obviously constructed as an afterthought, the room is a wide corridor divided length-wise by a waist-high counter on which is mounted a sheet of plexiglass. Talk holes have been punched in this sheet at regular intervals.

Margaret does not want to go near it. Behind her an ancient radiator gurgles out too much heat. Pea-green paint curls away from a water stain on the wall beside the radiator. Margaret unbuttons her coat, wonders for the hundredth time what she is doing here.

The door on the prisoners' side opens.

"Maggie!" Rodger's face registers surprise: he was expecting someone else... His mother probably. But now he is coming forward eagerly, so glad to see her, pathetically glad. "What are you doing here?"

"I don't know, I must be out of my mind. I took a week's holiday. I came on the bus, all the way across the prairies, as soon as I found out..." She tries to smile, but there are so many different feelings crashing about inside her.

He is smiling his beautiful smile as if there is no problem, damn his eyes. She takes the hardbacked chair on her side of the glass. He looks thin, sallow under these hideous fluorescent lights.

"Do they give you proper food in here?" she hears her voice asking.

He laughs.

"Excellent, better than some restaurants I could name... Remember the Bangor, Maggie?"

She has to smile.

They had dinner at the Bangor on an impulse. It was just after the war, their first time out together alone after Rodger could eat again and Little Charlie was born; it was also the first time they ever dined in a restaurant. Margaret unearthed the dress she was married in, they dropped Little Charlie off at Rodger's parents', and Rodger took ten dollars they could ill afford to the Bangor, "where two could dine with class for the price of one and a half."

Waiters gliding around the lamplit room reduced Margaret and Rodger to whispers. Also, one glance at the menu told them that in spite of the jingle, their ten dollars would be barely enough. Then the food arrived. Flamboyantly, the waiter lifted the silver domes covering their plates; it was not until he had withdrawn that Margaret noticed there was something wrong.

No steam was rising from the coat of gluey gravy spread across a lump she could only assume was roast beef. She looked across at the fricassee pasted to Rodger's plate.

"Why, I could do better than this at home!" Her voice, trilling its English cadences, pierced the hushed atmosphere. The waiter reappeared without a sound.

"Something wrong with Madam's dinner?"

"Yes, something is definitely wrong with Madam's dinner! It's stony cold, that's what, and—" Her glance happened to drop to his feet. "You're wearing slippers! That's why we can't hear you!" She dissolved into a fit of giggles...

Twenty-six years later, in Thunder Bay's jailhouse, Margaret finds herself laughing again. Then, seeing Rodger laughing with her, as if this miserable glass were not between them, as if everything was just fine, brings back the anger that has been with her for weeks, ever since Uncle Art and Aunt Bea arrived at her door in Vancouver.

"Why didn't you tell me about this, Rodger?" This more than anything is what hurts her. "Why did the boys and I have to find out second hand?"

He looks down.

"All these years, why in God's name couldn't you trust me enough to tell me?"

He raises his head in surprise.

"Trust you? No, no, it wasn't that..."

"What then?"

"Well it was just that I couldn't... I didn't want you to have to live with this."

"But we did have to live with it, every day, every night..." She looks at him sadly. "So many years, you cost us, Rodger... And this was why. When I left you that first time, I left my baby because I thought you would come after me, I thought..." She tries to blink away the tears. She has sworn to herself that she will not cry. But it still hurts so much, even though Little Rodger is a grown man now, a welder with a family of his own. "And then when you didn't come—"

"I started to, Maggie, right after you left. But then it— this— happened..." He looks through the glass at her. "I wanted you and Charlie back more than anything, and I was angry with you for leaving me and Little Rodg', for taking Charlie. For years I was, even after you came back, I was so angry with you. I wanted you back so bad... But then on my way to get you this happened and I couldn't remember." His fist hits the counter on his side, "I could not remember what happened! And there was so much guilt, I was sick with it, don't you see? I woke up that morning in Ottawa, and I didn't even know how I got there, then I saw the paper about the murder and... How could I ask you to come home?"

He turned up in England eventually, though. By then Margaret's mother and new friends had begun to soften the grief of losing her baby and her husband. She stopped expecting him to show up at any moment. She put Charlie into playschool and took up accounting. A fellow student called Gerald began to call on her.

Margaret and Gerald were having tea in her upstairs flat the first time Rodger showed up. He rang the bell, then called up the stairwell, and when she heard his voice her heart stopped. He joined them for tea. Gerald rose to leave but Rodger would not hear of it. He also did not appear to be able to sit still. Less than an hour later, before she could talk to him, discover anything at all, he went away again...

"I couldn't ask you to live with a murderer, could I? And I thought... well, that you would be better off..."

At first Margaret hated him. After a few months Gerald asked her to marry him. She was fond of Gerald, and life with only a small child for company was a lonely proposition. Also, Charlie needed a father and Gerald was a steady, Godfearing man. She started divorce proceedings.

When Rodger showed up again a year later, she took great pleasure in telling him about how she planned to marry Gerald, how good that would be for Charlie. But as Rodger nodded, agreeing with her, she saw his pain. Not just about this. Something was dreadfully wrong.

Rodger left again, and in the silence that followed her outpouring she realized that Gerald was a means to an end, nothing more. The man she loved was the one she had just finished divorcing. She sent Gerald away, determined that once her accounting course was finished she would earn enough money to go back to Vancouver. She would have Little Rodger back...

"If you thought I'd be better off without you, when I came back to Vancouver, why did you marry me all over again?"

"I couldn't believe my good luck! That day when I came into Mother's to get Little Rodg' and there you were sitting on the couch, I could not believe my eyes. It was my fantasy come true! And... well," he looks down at the counter top between them. "Once I had you back and we were finally a family again, I just didn't have the strength to give you up—"

"But you—"

"— I thought that maybe after all the years I had a right to forget the damned murder." Remembered anger raises his voice.

"But you didn't forget."

Night after night Margaret woke to find Rodger sitting up straight in the bed, shaking. But, "It's nothing," he would insist, snuggling down again, "just a stupid nightmare." Later, when the dream became more frequent he would try to escape it with pills, or by staying out late, coming home smelling of drink. Finally, he told her he was going back to sea.

If he did that again, she replied, he needn't bother coming back. "I have loved you, Rodger, but you cannot seem to live the married life. Less now than you ever could, it seems..."

"You let it destroy us, Rodger!" She says now, angry all over again, even after all these years.

He does not reply.

"Why didn't you just tell me?"

He looks at her, sees the years that lie between them, feels the safety of their distance.

"You would have insisted I go to the police, and if they had found me guilty... well, I just couldn't do that to you and the boys... Even if I had not been convicted..." He looks away.

"What? Do you think I would have skulked around the house, forever wondering if the father of my children was a murderer? Honestly, Rodger, who could possibly know you better than me?"

He sighs.

"I just thought it best to leave you and the boys alone, unscathed. To remain friends..." He hears the lameness in this, wonders if she knows the whole truth... "Please, Margaret, at least now I'm trying to do the right thing, find out the truth—"

"The right thing, the truth! Rodger, for God's sake, we were warm blooded human beings, the boys and I, we needed you, not right and truth..." It is Margaret's turn to sigh. "But you never have been able see that, have you?"

The old pain fills their silence.

"What about the boys?" Rodger asks at last, "Did they come with you?"

"No... But they're trying to understand, too."

Rodger nods. After a while he says, "Do you know... I don't suppose you've seen my mother?"

"Your mother. What does she have to do with all this?" Then suddenly, Margaret realizes that the old lady has a lot to do with this. Pictures in black and white— snapshots of the past— pop into her mind: the cold, unforgiving look on his mother's face when Margaret arrived, as if the fact that Rodger was in pieces was somehow her fault; his mother at the front door of the Vancouver brownstone, night after night, when Rodger's pain was too bad and Margaret needed help getting him back to the hospital; later, Rodger and his father glancing fearfully— yes fearfully!— in his mother's direction, while they discussed a night out with the boys; still later, after Margaret came back from England, the look of love in the hard old eyes as, unaware that she was being observed, she watched her younger grandson open his Christmas presents; and Little Rodger's instant obedience when she scolded him a moment later for throwing down the discarded wrapping paper... So much power the old lady wielded!

"She's here, but I haven't had a chance to see her since... since this. I just hope she's okay."

Margaret looks through the plexiglass at Rodger's worried face. Even now, in the middle of a murder trial that could ruin his life, the old woman has him thinking about her!

"Don't you worry one minute about your mother, she's fine. If you haven't seen her yet, it's just that she's tired." Who knows, maybe that's right. Maybe that is the only reason she's staying away from her own son when he's in trouble, when he obviously needs to see her. Margaret smiles: "She is seventy-seven, after all."

"Time, Mrs. Brown!" A middle-aged guard with a Scottish accent comes into view behind Rodger.

"The defense starts tomorrow," Rodger tells her. "Will you be there?"

She doesn't want to be, why should she be? After all the years, it's not as if she owes him anything.

"It's a little late, don't you think, Rodger?" But if that is so, she can see him thinking, then why has she come all this way? She buttons her coat, picks up her purse, so many feelings sucking her down, churning her round and round like one of those eddies you see below a waterfall. She looks through the glass at him: how can it be so, after all these years?

He smiles the same old smile.

"For old time's sake?" He puts his hand up through the talk hole. "It's good to see you, Margaret."

"Br-r-rown!" Touching is not allowed.

She hesitates. Sees the guard take a step towards them. Reaches out quickly to grasp Rodger's hand, just for a moment. Then goes quickly, before he can see that she is crying.

Surprisingly, she wants to talk. I put my throbbing foot up in one of the salmon pink booths at a nearby greasy spoon, and we stir our dishwater coffee in the lonely gloom of the November evening. She struggles to stop crying.

"So silly," she sniffs, putting her hankie away, "after all these years."

I had thought she would be a tough, brazen woman. After all, she had up and left her baby. But the soft English nuances of her voice, and the story she has been telling me about what happened to them all those years ago, and about tonight's visit, have long since banished that image.

"So," she finishes now, chuckling without humour, "it would seem that in spite of everything, and of all the years, I still care about the stupid bastard. Even though he left me. Twice..." She shakes her head. "What a fool I am."

"Margaret," I push back my hair, look into her grey eyes: who better than she knows the answer to my question? "Is he having us all on? I mean is this all one giant con?" I will be visiting him myself in a little while and I need a new framework for my questions, a way past the sympathy he is so good at inspiring.

"Of course it's a con. Haven't you figured out by now that all men are con artists? Everything, the whole world as we know it, has been set up and run by conning men: 'What's in it for me?' 'How can I be the winner, make someone else the loser?' Conning is the order of the day, my dear. Don't tell me you don't know that?"

I slump back in the booth, stir my grey coffee, listen to the clatter of the spoon against the thick white china.

"Right." Isn't this what my own fight is about, the reason I wear boots, no make-up, the reason I fled to Thunder Bay... A man's life, from what I've seen so far, revolves first and foremost around the man, and I will not play June Cleaver to my lover's Ward... I readjust my sore foot on the seat of the booth. I can't write John off, I haven't even spoken to him today. And he is a gentle, sweet, thoughtful man... So why am I so angry with him?

"More coffee?" The waitress waves the pot from the far side of the lunch counter. We nod, we are her only customers.

"And I'll have one of those too, please." I point at brick-thick chocolate brownies piled pyramid-style under a plastic dome on the counter.

"Me too," says Margaret. The waitress sets down the desserts and I sigh. "Why am I going to eat this? I'm not hungry, are you?" I eye the two brown slabs. "Barb, our Family Section editor just did a piece about how the real reason women eat has nothing to do with hunger."

Margaret chuckles, takes a huge bite.

"She's right."

We munch companionably. Then:

"I'm through with men," Margaret declares.

I look at her.

"Really," she takes a last bite of brownie, "after Rodger and I broke up the second time I swore off men for good... Oh, I'm not saying I don't know any men. I just know them on my terms now." The grey eyes Rodger fell for all those years ago reflect a kind of pain, but also a ferocity, and a flame of joy I know nothing about.

I do not know what to say.

"You have a man?" She is smiling. This no longer seems to be a newspaper interview.

I sip my coffee. It scalds my tongue, bringing tears to my eyes. I nod.

"But he's not here. He lives in Ottawa. We see each other about every other weekend."

"Ah, clever girl!" She is delighted. "Just don't you go and ruin it by marrying him, whatever you do."

I smile, nodding again. But surely, I think to myself, there must be some way that married life can include both love and equal freedom for the woman?

ᘓ CHAPTER 9 ᘔ

...The car is fishtailing wildly, its headlights strafing the frozen bush like the crazed eyes of some other-world Goliath. Rodger grips the armrest, trying to stay upright, to keep the bottle in his hand from spilling. The car stops and now the figures, muffled in black robes this time, are coming towards the car, their mouths— black holes— opening and closing as they come closer, closer, pointing. And now one of them is pounding on the roof right over Rodger's head. Another peers in at the window, still mouthing something, accusing him, and this time the face, oddly elongated through the glass, is recognizable—

"Br-r-rown!"

Rodger starts, finds himself on his cot. He must have dozed off. He blinks, trying to orient himself, to place a new, lingering, sickening sense of recognition. Remembers: the face in the dream is Richardson's.

You son of a bitch, he tells the face, you used me. And all the time I thought... Rodger rubs the bridge of his nose.

"Brown, you are a popular fellow this evening. That reporter girl is back." The door to his cell clangs open.

He won't see me. He is too tired.

"Well?" The jailor tonight is Harry, a youngish man with a wife and two toddlers at home. "You comin', or what?"

Rodger looks around his cell. The air in here is stale, full of the aftermath of the nightmare. He'll never get back to sleep. He forces himself to his feet.

He looks played out, I think when he comes in. Maybe I should go, leave him alone.

Or maybe I should use the opportunity to break through his facade of politeness, good will... I smile.

"Are you sure you want to do this?"

"Sure," he shrugs. "Why not? I have a few minutes to spare... You're limping."

"Yeah, I ran into a table." I switch on the tape recorder, go straight to the point.

"Rodger, you told Inspector Richardson you shot Boucher. 'I shot him,' you said. You also told the other cops the same thing. Why did you say that, if the truth is you don't know?"

Rodger sighs.

"That, dear girl, is the sixty-four-thousand-dollar question... All I can say is that there was so much more I told them, too. So much that jury never heard."

I want to nod, to support him, be his friend. But I am a reporter. I steel myself, shake out a cigarette, offer it to him, light us both.

"But either you shot the man, or you didn't shoot the man, right? And if you don't know for sure that you did shoot him, why did you tell Richardson you did?"

Rodger takes a long drag on his cigarette, exhales, shaking his head, thinking it out as he speaks.

"All I can say is that I needed to talk about it, get it out into words in a court of law so that it could be cleared up, once and for all... Richardson was helping me and... the blood and the snow and the corpse in the dream have always seemed so real...

"But the truth is that I don't know if I shot the man. I might have... But Richardson knows damned well that I don't know, the bastard!– pardon me, miss– so, why is he so hot to convict me all of a sudden?"

"He obviously thinks you did it." I slouch in my chair, my jean-clad legs stretched out under the table. It's late, suddenly I'm tired, and my foot is still throbbing. This tiny, fluorescent-lit, tiled room is pretty dismal at 9:30 p.m. "Maybe he thinks your dream is really memory—"

"No!"

I look across the table at him.

"Well, if what you say is true, isn't that really why you came here? To see if the dream does point to the truth, if that's why it's been preying on you all these years?"

Rodger closes his eyes.

"Is that the reason you never told Margaret?" I ask gently. "Because you were afraid it was true?"

The tube lights buzz in the silence, the tape recorder hums. Then, finally, Rodger opens his eyes, sighs.

"'You let it destroy us, Rodger,' that's what she told me tonight. 'Why couldn't you trust me enough to tell me?'... Elsa said it was destroying us, too." He sighs again and I watch him realize a new piece of the truth.

"There have been so many women since Margaret, some I married, some I didn't, but none of them lasted and in the end I'd always wind up back at sea... A man is safe at sea. You have your bunk and your meals and a job to do, and when the ship docks you can go ashore and explore all these strange places, hear the languages, smell the air, taste the foods... or you can stay on your bunk and read... So after a while that's what I did.

"Then, two years ago, I met Elsa. And now, for the first time in all the years, I know what it is to really love a woman. Margaret I cared for. I... made love to Margaret, but I don't think I ever truly loved her, with all of my soul. Not the way I love Elsa, not so that what mattered to me most in the whole world was what was happening inside her, you know?

"And that's why, when the apprenticeship turned out so deadly dull, and Little Charlie kept on waking up crying in the middle of every night, and Margaret was so sad all the time because of homesickness and her father's death, and it seemed like everybody needed something from me, that's why I started watching the seagulls, then finally got a ship, flew the coop..."

"There was nothing there to hold me to the grindstone, see? Nothing but duty and guilt... I really didn't have a clue what love was, then."

"So it was guilt that kept you from telling Margaret about the murder?" Do I believe any of this? Is he as genuine as he sounds?

"Well, I guess so... But I did really care for her and Little Charlie too, I mean it hurt so bad to lose them... Oh, hell," he sweeps away his confusion, "I don't know, it's all too complicated for this tiny brain."

I stare at him, recognizing the pattern his thinking has taken all these years: get close to the point, too close for comfort, then give up, shy away, make a joke and leave, all the strings tangled, undone... He wants to get to the heart of the matter, but he's also afraid to, and he does not know how to think his way past the fear... I know the feeling.

I sit up straight. Could it be that all he needs is a sounding board, and the right kind of guidance?

"It might not be so complicated."

"Huh?" He has been staring at his fingernails. Now he reaches across the table, takes another cigarette out of my pack. "May I?" He offers one to me, lights us both.

"You might be able to clear all this up yourself," I tell him. "You could start with the dream. I'll help you. We could compare the dream to the information you have heard in court, see if they match. If they do, the dream is probably memory. If they don't—"

Rodger is already shaking his head, pulling on the cigarette, afraid.

"— Why not? You came here looking for the truth, didn't you?" It is a challenge: show me this isn't all bullshit.

He smokes for a while. Then stubs out the butt.

"Okay," he shrugs, "I might as well give her a whirl."

I struggle to contain my exhilaration. I am an explorer heading towards virgin territory.

"Okay, let's start with the car ride in the dream. Describe it."

He nods.

"Right... We are barrelling along a bumpy road and it is snowing..."

"Chestleman, the snowplough driver, said it was snowing. And he described the frozen bumps on the road."

"So that could be why the car in the dream is fishtailing and I have to hang on..." Rodger looks depressed, "but how could I know that unless I was there?"

"What about the car in the dream: is it a taxi? Is there blood on the seat?"

Rodger thinks hard.

"I don't know. In the dream I am looking outside the car... The taxi driver is not in the car, he is already dead..."

"Who is the driver, then?"

"...He is a large person, much larger than me."

"French Canadian? Is he wearing a Hudson's Bay coat?"

Rodger tries to focus.

"...There is no detail in the dream."

"Okay then, let's try the body."

Rodger sighs.

"That's the rub. In the dream it's lying in the ditch behind the snowbank just like that snowplough operator said. And the head wound is the same, a bullet hole. He looks the same in the photographs as he does in the dream, except that he is standing up in the dream... and there is more snow."

"It snowed the night of the murder."

"Yes."

"Is there a wallet in the dream, a watch?"

Rodger brightens.

"No. Do you think that counts for anything?"

"I don't know. Is there a gun?"

"No." But he looks away from me. I smoke for a while.

"You can tell me all of it, you know. We're not in court now... So, let's try your real memory now: see if the bits you actually remember about that night match the dream and the court evidence. Maybe you can fit it all together that way."

"I doubt that, I've only been trying for twenty-five years."

"Come on, we're doing great. Start at the beginning of the trip east, with the train from Calgary."

He gives me a quizzical look: what makes you think you can help... or that I should trust you? The glare from the fluorescent lighting bleaches the colour out of his face, accentuates the shadows under his eyes.

I meet his look head on. The exploration is heading up now, into mountains not even Cosselli has climbed. I am afraid: what if he cracks? What if something happens way out here that I cannot handle? What if he tells me something...? But I am not about to turn back.

"What have you got to lose?"

He plays with his fingernails, then finally, he waves at the tape recorder.

"Turn that damned thing off."

"Right! Now, just let your mind go. Take yourself back twenty-five years to the Calgary railway station. Tell me about the train ride."

He nods, looks up over my shoulder at a water stain on the wall near the ceiling.

"It is cold, April. I am sitting on a leather passenger seat, wearing Uncle Art's tweed suit. The extra pants are in my duffel bag, stowed up on the luggage rack, and out the window I can see the little puffs of breath as Uncle Art and Aunt Bea talk to each other..."

The train lurches forward, the wheels shrieking, metal against metal, as they begin to roll, and his uncle and aunt are waving and smiling at him.

He waves back, feeling so good. He has been able to talk things over with them in a way he never could at home, and somehow that has purified him. He has a new sense of purpose.

She would not be sorry, he had promised Margaret that the morning after their wedding, and by God she will not be. He will find her in England and explain why his ship was delayed for so long and then together they will lay out a new, better plan.

The hills to the east are snowless, the treeless landscape soft and brown as an animal's hide until suddenly, around Medicine Hat, it breaks up into gorges, coolies carved thousands of years ago by some river's folly. In their reaches, if you look hard, you can find white-tailed deer standing near the roaming cattle and, closer to the track but less visible, rabbits and the dainty white and faun antelope. The afternoon wears on and the earth flattens. Only the occasional leaning cabin in the fields testifies that the cattle belong to someone. Sloughs, like giant sequins on the flat prairie, mirror the pink sunset sky, then the mirror shatters as a wood duck or a flock of Canada geese glide in to land. The dusk deepens and the train's call becomes a lonely, haunted sound. The strangers inside the passenger car, familiar to each other after the long day, draw closer together, conversations becoming freer, more intimate, familial.

A little girl in a red dress, the youngest of a large Italian-speaking family, sets out to explore the aisle. She is about four. She stops beside Rodger's seat, fixes huge soulful eyes on him. They jolt him at first, the same way it jolts him when anyone touches the scars across his belly, until he gets used to it. But then the little girl laughs, anchoring him squarely in the present and, laughing with her, he breaks the stick of gum he was about to chew in half, hands her a share.

Rodger sleeps sitting up, his head resting against the extra suit pants, bunched up into a pillow, wakes to the sounds of raindrops spattering the window. Outside, dirty puddles are spreading like plague spots across a snow-covered prairie. Lone poplars, shorn of their leaves, stand like stragglers lost on a barren landscape, all that is left of some fleeing population of trees. And who would not flee this place? It is so different from yesterday, as if, like Alice, they have passed through a looking glass.

They come into Winnipeg late in the afternoon. It is still raining.

"Bye, mister!" The little girl in the red dress waves from the end of a string of children further up the platform. Grinning, Rodger waves back. He still feels so good, in spite of the rain.

He is supposed to stop here to work. He can get day jobs in the mines, make enough easily to pay his fare to the east coast. But there, right in front of him, an eastbound freight train lies like a serpent, hissing steam. He could jump it, keep right on going, out of this hideous freezing place.

A lineman lights a light standard further up the track. It shows Rodger an open boxcar door. He looks around. There are no guards. The lineman's back disappears into the rainy dusk.

Rodger runs down the line, heaves his duffle bag, then himself into the boxcar. Sits there catching his breath, smiling into the darkness. The gods are definitely with him today. By tomorrow he will be halfway across Ontario.

Then something stirs in the front end of the car. He is not alone. He sits perfectly still. He can see nothing, but now he can hear whispering. Then the floor under him shakes. He scrambles to his feet.

An enormous man shuffles into view. He is over six feet tall and heavyset. He is wearing a light-coloured coat and high leather boots. Rodger cannot read his face in the gloom, but there is a smell of cheap wine. In his hand the big man carries a bag out of which sticks the neck of a bottle.

"Salut!" Throwing back his head, he takes a swig, holds the bag out to Rodger. "Prends-en!"

Sociability seems the safest course. The wine's tinny sweetness slides down Rodger's throat.

"Merci, mon ami," he jokes, resurrecting the French he picked up in Europe. He hands the bottle back.

"Ah, tu parles français, toi! Eh, Joey," Mountain Man looks back over his shoulder, "il parle français. Viens, toi, viens t'assoir!" The man beckons to Rodger, then lumbers back into the darkness. "Eh, light us a match, Joey."

The flame catches, flares, and in its light Rodger sees a small rat-faced man sitting against the wall. He is surrounded by bottles, some empty, some still in their paper bags.

"Where did you get all that booze?"

A string of rapid French, hostile as machine gun fire, issues from Rat Face. Mountain Man laughs, "You don't mind him, drink!"

Rodger hesitates. Mountain Man sways over him.

Well maybe just one, he decides, for courtesy's sake. Besides, the evening world outside is cold and wet. A drink of wine might help him sleep. He sits down. Mountain Man drops down beside him, jarring the boxcar. He takes a long swig from the bottle then, passing it to Rodger, begins to sing:

"Prendre un petit gout c'est agréable..." His baritone is rich. After a few swigs, Rat Face adds a thin soprano:

"Prendre un petit gout, c'est doux..." Then they are both gesturing to Rodger, teaching him the words:

"Prendre un petit gout, ça rends l'esprit malade..." The acoustics inside the boxcar are marvellous, almost as good as a shower. Rodger takes another swig of wine and, as the song ends and a new one begins, another. Why not? There is nothing else to do in here, nowhere else he has to go tonight...

But they did go somewhere.

"The wine must have run out," Rodger guesses now, "because we left the boxcar to go to a hotel across the street from the railway station. We met the shoe salesman there, he drove us to Geraldton... And it was a long ride and so cold—

"Wait a minute!" Rodger sits up straight. "In the tape I told Richardson I was in the back seat with a jug of wine. And in the dream I am always in the back. I was also in the back of the shoe salesman's car, that I do know... Could the ride I told Richardson about, and the ride in the dream, be that ride, before we even got to Geraldton? The road would have been frozen and it could have been snowing... It was snowing. If this is so, it explains why there is no wallet, no broken watch in my memory... Maybe it even explains the strange blood on my pants!"

"Maybe. But keep going now." I am leaning forward across the table, "There is more memory, isn't there?"

Rodger stares at me, then sighs, deflated.

"Yeah, there is more. I... I've never told this part to anyone..." He takes a breath, forces the memory into focus. His voice becomes a monotone.

"We are in a hotel room, it must have been in Geraldton. It's the kind of room that has an iron bedstead and hanging light bulb, last year's squished flies still stuck to the walls. We have to stay, curse the shoe salesman— there are no night trains out of Geraldton. Then our wine runs out again. So we go downstairs to a bar in the hotel basement. The salesman is no longer with us...

"The bar is noisy and jammed full of men. It's so smoky you can hardly see. We are sitting around, still drinking, when suddenly Mountain Man starts waving a gun around. It is a service revolver, a .38. I tell him to put the damned thing away. I am not surprised to see the gun; like the detective said in the courtroom, there are all kinds of guns around. Guys have brought them back from the war and never turned them in or registered them... But I am afraid, the big guy is drunk as a skunk by now. We all are.

"'Put it away,' I tell him again.

"'Non, non,' he waves the thing around in the air. 'We need some money.' He leans down, close between Rat Face and me.

"'We could go rob a bank. Take a cab to the next town, rob us a bank, eh?' His breath is heavy with the stench of old food and cheap wine. 'We leave 'dis town right away. Nobody ever know us... Get some cash! You in, Brown?'

"'Sounds good to me,' I said."

"You said that?" I am there in the bar with him, breathing the stale, wine-sweet air, smelling the sweat of a room full of lumber-jacks.

"Well, sure. I told you, I was three sheets over the windmill. Whatever anyone said sounded good. Also, this son of a bitch was twice my size, remember, and I'm not even sure I can stand up by now."

"So what happened?"

Rodger puts a hand over his eyes, rubs his forehead.

"Come on, Rodger."

He opens his eyes, surveys me, then, reaching a decision, straightens his back in the chair, forces himself back into the hotel bar.

The memory becomes a feeling now, of the wine taking over his body. It is warm, its colours swirling behind his eyes, so beautiful... Then someone is shaking his shoulder.

"You come now, Anglais."

"What? Where?"

"We go take a cab. East. You come."

But the bottle on the table is not quite empty.

"Uh-uh," he shakes his head, "Not while there's a drink left..."

I wait. Rodger sighs.

"So?" I ask finally, "Did you drink the last drink?"

Rodger shakes his head.

"I don't know, I think I must have done... I can't imagine that I wouldn't have, at that point."

"And? Then what?"

"Nothing."

"What do you mean, nothing?" I wait. "You mean that's the end of your memory?"

He nods once, decisively.

Whatever the truth is, the door to his willingness has just closed.

"Well, hey," I sit back, relax. "We've done pretty well so far, don't you think? We now have possible explanations for the wild car ride and the frozen road in your dream, also for your knowledge of the large French Canadian in the Hudson's Bay coat and of the service revolver."

He looks at me, interested.

"Also, I looked on a map. If you woke up in Ottawa, you could not have taken the rail route south via Nipigon to Toronto and on to Montreal, as you told Lucas in '47. Therefore, since there were no night trains, you may have left Geraldton by car... You definitely were in the wrong place at the wrong time... But as to whether or not you were actually present at the scene of the murder..."

"There is the corpse in the snowbank in my dream," he reminds me.

"True. But you were questioned in '47. Maybe you saw the photos then... The only thing is, 'There was so much blood,' you told Richardson. What blood is that?"

"I wish I knew. But all I can see is the blood splashing out of someone's head..."

"The cab driver's head?"

"I honestly don't know... There is just blood, so much blood..."

He looks down but I see that his jawline is quivering.

And suddenly I remember that this mountainscape I am exploring is the inside of another person's mind, a place I know nothing whatever about— except that a person's psyche can be as delicate as frost, as full of lethal fissures as a glacier. How dare I trespass here! Suddenly I am unnerved.

Back down slowly, gently, I tell myself. And smile.

"Well, don't forget that your pants had some unrelated person's blood on them. Maybe you got into some other scrap... Or maybe you did sell the pants. Maybe someone else threw them off the train. Maybe you hitched a ride to Ottawa alone."

"But I woke up in the Ottawa freightyard. I had to go to Hearst to catch a freight to Ottawa."

"Well then, maybe the French Canadian did wait for you to finish your wine, and maybe you did get into the cab with him and drive to Hearst. The cab was found outside Hearst with Boucher's blood all over it. Maybe the French Canadian shot Boucher. That's why you remember the blood..."

"...Maybe."

A thought strikes me. "You have a clear memory of blood, so much blood. Don't you think that if you had shot a man in the head, you would remember that clearly, too?"

"I don't know... I remember waking up beside the tracks in the railyard, so stiff I could hardly walk. I was numb. Another hour or so and I'm sure I would have frozen to death..." He gives me his rueful grin. "Maybe it's too bad I didn't... I was alone. So I stumbled across the road into this greasy spoon, and ordered a coffee. There was a newspaper there on the counter, and that's where I read about the murder in Geraldton. I felt so bad, just so terrible. I don't think I have ever felt so awful, so low in my life, and it's not the only bender I've been on..."

"So you knew you had been there."

Rodger hesitates, then nods. We have made it safely back to where I can feel the hard, familiar ground beneath my feet. I take a deep breath.

"You know, Rodger, you really should tell all this stuff to Cosselli."

"I did. Well, not like we did tonight, not putting it all together, but—"

"So tell him what we just did. I think he believes you're holding out on him. So give him all the facts—"

"Facts!" Rodger snorts. "Since when are facts going to help me? Who's going to believe I can remember as much as I do, but not the one big moment?... They'll think I'm blocking out the fatal moment, or that—"

"Or that you don't remember it because you were not there. The point of this whole murder trial is that you don't know which is true either, do you? That's why you have to get all of it out, all of it! So that the court's decision on this murder will be based on everything, the whole truth as you know it. That's what you want, isn't it?"

"What I did want, fool that I was: the whole truth. But who in that courtroom cares anything about the whole truth? Not Richardson, that's for sure, and not that prosecutor. They're out to get me. And not Cosselli either, the way he monkeyed around with that 1947 statement of mine... The way I see it now, the truth has bugger all to do with this."

It is midnight. I sit at my kitchen table, my sore foot propped up on a chair, sipping my way through a pot of tea, and staring at the notes I have made.

Facts, the truth. Rodger is wrong, they do have something more than "bugger all" to do with his trial... But what, exactly?

"Intent, that's the key to our justice system," Cosselli has told me. "With a crime like murder, the law demands proof of intent:

"A car runs over a man and kills him, for instance. Did the driver intend to kill the man? If so, the act is murder. If not, maybe it's manslaughter, or criminal negligence causing death, or maybe just an unavoidable accident. Foss decides which charge to lay, then he has to establish not only the facts, but also the accused person's frame of mind, or intentions, at the time the criminal act happened."

The pages of notes blur in front of my eyes. Enough for tonight, I should go to bed. My brain is mush. Maybe I will just phone John first, say goodnight...

But still I sit there, thinking of Rodger, the way he would look away from me at certain points tonight. He has told me a lot, more than any reporter has any right to hear... But not all of it, of that I am certain.

So who knows what his intentions were that night?

Richardson thinks Rodger's intention, upon calling the R.C.M.P. in Vancouver, was to confess... I rub my eyes, and a new thought swims up out of the murky confusion. How can you ever prove intent? Doesn't the way things look differ according to the perspectives of the judge, the lawyers, the jury on any given day?

My mind, the bonds of its Anglo-Saxon logic loosened by exhaustion, throws up the picture of the eighteen-year-old native boy who axed his uncle to death. How did intent figure there? The ugly bugger was going to rape the boy's mother, who was defenseless. If she had axed him herself— which was impossible— she probably would have got off, the intent being self-defense... But her son had to do it for her. His intent was defense, too, but the court's view had been coloured by the amount of drink they had all consumed, the suggestion being that had the boy been sober, the death would not have happened. There would have been another way out of the situation. And so he was found guilty of a criminal act.

Was that right or wrong, just or unjust? I rub my eyes, I have no idea. But suddenly the carriage of justice seems to me a very shaky affair, dependent upon so many iffy propositions, so many people's biases: like everything else in my life... Not something I would want to count upon.

CHAPTER 10

Bertie the bailiff opens the door and Rodger scans the courtroom, looking for his mother. Hundreds of eyes, cold, inquisitive, look back at Rodger. He hurries towards the prisoner's dock.

"Peter?" Cosselli is tensed over his notes. "Peter!" Cosselli turns. "Have you seen my mother this morning? Is she all right?"

"No," Cosselli looks surprised. "I haven't seen anybody yet." Rising, he scans the body of the courtroom. Uncle Art pushes his way up the crowded aisle, offers Rodger his hand.

"How are you, son?"

"Okay, I guess. Where's Mother?"

"She's fine, she's just resting. Bea says she's tired, too, so I left the two of them back at the hotel." The old man is not a good liar.

"She's okay, though?"

Uncle Art nods. "She's a tough old bird."

"Yeah," Cosselli chuckles.

"She hasn't gone home?"

"No, no, she's not going anywhere."

"She's just sleeping in, Rodg'," Cosselli claps him on the shoulder, "she knows we've got the defense wrapped up."

But his mother hasn't come all this way to stay in a hotel room.

"Get her to come soon, will you Uncle Art? She needs to hear my defense."

His uncle pats his arm.

"I'll try."

Cosselli peers at Rodger.

"You all right, sport?"

"What? Yeah, I'm fine... Only there is one little thing, Peter... You did ask me if there was anything I haven't told you and... well—"

The door at the front of the court, beside the judge's bench, opens. Cosselli turns towards it, signals Rodger to keep quiet.

"But it's important, Peter!"

"Later then, tell me at the lunch recess." Cosselli moves back to his place at the table.

The full courtroom rises for the judge, waits, sits down with a shuffling of feet, a clearing of throats. Then:

"My Lord," Cosselli begins, "the defense will call two witnesses on the *voir dire*."

R.C.M.P. Constable Kilgore's young partner, Constable Terrence Flowers, is visibly nervous. Gently Cosselli leads him back into the Vancouver bar: "How many beers did you see the accused drink?"

Constable Flowers stands up straight.

"He may have taken a swig from the glass in front of him, but that was all."

"What did he look like?"

"He was very upset, red in the face, and his eyes were glassy from crying."

"Was he intoxicated, in your view?"

"No, sir." Flowers appears to brace himself. Cosselli smiles.

"Now, Constable, we have established that when you took Mr. Brown out to the car, he was technically under arrest. Were you restraining him physically in any way?"

"Oh, no, sir, he was more than willing to come."

"So you never touched him at all."

"No, sir..." Flowers hesitates, "at least not to keep him from running away."

"How then?"

"Well, sir, it was nothing... Just that as we came out of the hotel I was walking beside him and he missed his step. So I reached out and caught hold of his arm, that's all."

"He missed his step?" Cosselli's voice is quiet.

"Yes, sir, he just stumbled slightly."

"He stumbled? Why? Was there an unexpected step?"

"No, sir, it was just... he tripped."

"Tripped. There was a crack in the pavement, was there?"

"No, sir, at least I don't know if there was... he just tripped a little. It was nothing."

"Oh?" Cosselli cocks his head. "Constable, isn't unsteadiness on the feet usually a sign of impairment?"

There is a pause.

"Yes, sir, it can be."

"So, he was glassy-eyed, red in the face. He drank in front of you, and he stumbled... Are you certain he was not at all impaired?"

"Sir... I..." Flowers' finger runs up and down the railing around the witness box. He is so easy to trap, it's almost pathetic. "I can only say that at the time we did not consider him to be impaired."

"Constable, how long have you been a member of the R.C.M.P.?"

"One year and eight months, sir."

"One year. That's not very long, is it? Now, at the station, Constable Kilgore went off to telex Ontario. What did you and Mr. Brown do while you waited for him?"

"Well, mostly I just tried to keep him calm, find out something about him. He was very nervous."

"And did he tell you anything, where he lived, for example?" Cosselli begins to pace in front of the table, apparently absorbed in his own thoughts.

"No, sir."

DEAD AND LIVING

"Wasn't that strange? A man is willing to bare his soul about a murder, but then will not give you his address?"

"He said he was worried about his family. He did not want them to know about this. He didn't want to hurt them any more, he said."

"And what did you reply, to try and calm him?"

"I told him they would probably not have to become involved." Foss, who has been writing notes, glances up sharply. Cosselli shows no emotion.

"Now, let me make sure I understand you. Brown— Jones as he was known to you then— said he did not want his family to know about the murder and you told him they would probably not have to become involved. Is that correct?"

Flowers glances apprehensively at Foss.

"Yes, sir, I just—"

"And how did Mr. Jones respond to that?"

"He seemed relieved."

"It set his mind at ease." Cosselli walks over to the lawyers' table to look at his notes. "Now, Constable, did the subject of the murder itself come up during your little chat?"

"Yes, sir, it did."

"And what did Mr. Jones say about that?"

Flowers glances down at a piece of paper in his hand.

"He repeated his story from the bar, only this time he said first that a French Canadian who was travelling with him had done it. Then he started to cry and said, 'No, that's wrong, why should I blame him?'"

Rodger looks down at his hands.

"Constable, I see that you are referring to a piece of paper," says Cosselli.

"Yes, sir." But Flowers looks uncomfortable.

159

"May I see it, please?" Cosselli advances on the witness stand. Flowers removes the paper from sight, a small boy caught red-handed.

"They aren't real notes, sir," he says quickly. "Not in my notebook. It's just a few lines I wrote down later to remind myself of what he said about the murder."

"May I see it, please." Cosselli's voice is that of a parent. Reluctantly, the constable hands him a half sheet of lined paper.

"There are only three sentences written here."

"Well as I said, I just wanted to recall what I thought was important—"

"What you thought was important! What about this court, Mr. Flowers? Is it to be allowed only to know about the three lines you want to recall from your conversation with the accused?"

"Objection!" Foss shoots to his feet. "Defense counsel is badgering his own witness, My Lord!"

"Sustained." Mr. Justice Harley looks down at Cosselli.

"I beg the court's pardon, My Lord," the defense lawyer replies. "It's just that I can't help wondering why an inexperienced constable would take it upon himself to deem what is and what is not important." Cosselli's contempt for the witness is more than showmanship.

Whatever the truth is, tough Kilgore and his side-kick Flowers are incompetent. That much is now obvious. So, does that mean that what we have heard through them, the 'I shot him' confession and so on, are lies, or only part of the truth, taken out of context by the police? Somebody seems to be lying here, but maybe it isn't Rodger after all.

Colour has spread across R.C.M.P. Constable Terrence Flowers' cheeks.

"Sir, I wasn't making notes for the court—"

"But you use them in court, don't you? You pass them off as the truth," Cosselli tosses the offending paper back to Flowers, turns his back to return to his seat. "I have no more questions of this witness."

Foss gives the constable a moment to regain his composure, then hooks his fingers into his waistcoat pockets.

"Constable, this 'chat' you had with the accused, did it take any particular course, or was it just a series of comments back and forth?"

"It was just casual comment."

"And was there any change in the accused's attitude towards the murder, or towards being at the station and making a statement, when you told him his family would probably not be involved?"

"No, sir, none at all," Flowers replies, relieved. "He was still nervous, chain-smoking a lot, looking around him all the time."

"Do you mean that he wanted to leave?"

"Oh, no, sir, quite the contrary. He was very anxious to clear the thing up."

"And in your opinion would he have left if you had not reassured him with regard to his family?"

"No, sir. He was there because he wanted to be there."

Foss nods and smiles.

"Thank you, Constable, that will be all."

Cosselli stands. "My Lord, the defense calls Dr. Michael Pryce!"

Rodger smiles.

"So you think I'm a loonybird?" Rodger asked when Cosselli told him a forensic psychiatrist would be coming from Toronto to see him. "No, no, not at all," Cosselli reassured him. "It's just that people sometimes do things, say things, and they have no idea why... I'd like you to talk to him, that's all."

So the slim, impeccably dressed Englishman sat across the table from Rodger in the lawyers' room at the jail and his grey hair, carefully trimmed, and wire rimmed glasses put Rodger on his guard at first, so that he didn't even smoke without asking permission.

But then Dr. Pryce put away his papers and they just talked, and as the hours wore on and the man with his quiet English accent sat smoking his pipe, filling the air with a sweet smelling cloud of smoke, Rodger found himself relaxing.

"Rodger Pearse Brown is an episodic alcoholic, in my view," Dr. Pryce tells the court. "Also an alcoholic amnesiac. This means that he drinks in bouts and after a certain point, he blanks out. I also found him to possess a strict moral code— that is, an unusually highly developed conscience that is linked to a deep regard for his family."

"An unusually highly developed conscience," says Cosselli. "Just how would this affect him in everyday life, Dr. Pryce?"

"Well, it means he has an unusually meticulous view of right and wrong which he sticks to... He would tend to judge his own behaviour very critically, so that where you or I might shrug off a dubious action with only a touch of remorse, a person with this character trait would suffer much more severely."

Rodger twists around to look back into the courtroom: where is his mother? She should be hearing this!

"Is this an illness? Are you saying this man is insane?"

"No, no, having a conscience of this kind is not an illness, it's more like having an exaggerated personality trait."

"You mean it's like a person having an unusually large nose: it's not a disease, but it still hurts like hell when it gets caught in a door."

Back in the body of the courtroom, the beast *Curiosity* titters. I am scribbling quickly, trying to catch every word.

Dr. Pryce has inclined his head.

"If you like."

"Now, what about the alcoholism?"

"Well, we know that excessive drinking is not always due to a physical addiction. Sometimes it is the result of a person's lack of ability to cope with stressful circumstances."

"You mean that if the circumstances in an unaddicted person's life changed, or if the person did not possess the personality traits he does, there might not be a drinking problem? Just as if the person with the large nose had not gone near the door, the headache could have been avoided?"

"My Lord," Foss is bored. "I fail to see what all these references to noses have to do with this trial."

"I beg the court's pardon," says Cosselli before Mr. Justice Harley can intervene, "I was just trying to establish a clear layman's understanding... Dr. Pryce, can you tell us what kind of alcoholic Mr. Brown is?"

"All the signs point to his being one of those for whom drinking has provided an escape."

Cosselli strokes his upper lip.

"That's very interesting... But what about this conscience of his, Doctor? Why wouldn't it stop him from drinking?"

"Well, there would be nothing morally wrong with taking a drink, he could easily talk himself into that. Also, it is important to bear in mind that a man with a rigid moral code doesn't necessarily always live up to the exigencies of that code. He might try to escape his conscience instead... So he would take another drink, and another. But when he woke up from one of these bouts, the conscience would make him feel extremely guilty."

"And? How does the amnesia fit into all this?"

The courtroom is completely quiet. Even the beast appears to have stopped breathing.

"Well, he would not remember anything. He would feel that he had done something terribly wrong, but he would not know what. And his conscience would demand to know. So he would think and search, almost to the point of obsession... As I have said, this kind of person, to whom right and wrong are of paramount importance, tends to feel guilt terribly strongly."

"I see," Cosselli nods. "Now, Dr. Pryce, let's go back to the circumstances in which Rodger Pearse Brown was embroiled during his trip east in April, 1947. How would all these factors have affected him then?"

"My Lord, I must object," says Foss, half rising. "Testimony of this kind would constitute only the merest speculation."

"My Lord, Dr. Pryce has been studying forensic psychiatry for twenty years," Cosselli argues. "He has spent several hours testing and interviewing my client, and I believe the court should have the full benefit of the conclusions of all that expertise."

Mr. Justice Harley nods.

"You'll have your turn, Mr. Foss. You may answer the question, Dr. Pryce."

"Thank you, My Lord... I can, of course, only surmise about Mr. Brown's condition in 1947, but after talking to him at length, it is my belief that when he woke up in Ottawa and read the newspaper, he may well have begun to wonder: 'If I was in Geraldton, did I do that murder? Is that the reason I feel so terribly badly?'"

I take a moment to look at Rodger. He is listening intently.

"Do you mean to say his guilt would have been strong enough to suggest murder, even if he had not done the murder?" Cosselli asks incredulously.

"Oh, yes, especially if he had been in the vicinity, so that the name of the place rang a bell. Once he had made the connection between himself and Geraldton, he would begin to believe that because he had been there, and because he felt so guilty, he must have committed the murder."

"So an innocent man could make himself believe he had done a murder?"

"Certainly. Fabricated memories are common enough with certain types of psychological disturbance."

"But he had no criminal record, no history of any kind of violence. How could he believe himself capable of murder?"

"Sir, a man who has operated his whole life according to conscience, who has spent all his life striving to do right— or running away from the necessity of that striving— often has no idea at all about who he is and what he is capable of. All he knows is that he has slipped way down the slippery slope, as it were..."

Rodger is leaning forward now, his face a study in concentration. The silence in the courtroom is broken only by the sound of my ballpoint racing across the page of my press pad.

"Now, Dr. Pryce," Cosselli continues, "suppose the accused did become convinced that he had done the murder. What would a man with Mr. Brown's personality and moral make-up do then?"

"Well, sir, once he attached his guilt to the murder, the belief would become more and more entrenched. He would begin to incorporate any facts that came his way through the newspapers or the police interview about his pants, for example, into what he came to think of as his memory."

"I see. And when would he do this, Doctor? Right away?"

"No, he might not have done it right away. At first the newspaper article might simply have kept recurring to him until gradually he came to believe that yes, he must have been there, then that yes, he had been there, then finally that yes, he did do the murder. That is why he has felt so guilty. In this case the whole process has taken twenty-five years. He may not have come to believe that 'yes, I am the one who did it,' until a few years ago...

"He obviously thought he had done it, or he would not have gone to the police, but the recall is not there." The psychiatrist looks over his bi-focals at Rodger. "The real source of the overwhelming guilt he felt may have been simply his drinking."

"Incredible," whispers someone in the courtroom.

"How would you go about identifying a fabricated memory such as you describe, Doctor?" Cosselli asks.

"Well, lack of knowledge about details, the absence of whole areas of fact are usually indications."

Cosselli nods.

"Doctor, you have examined the transcript of Mr. Brown's taped interview with Inspector Richardson. In your opinion are his answers on the tape consistent with a false memory?"

"Absolutely. There is the evidence of confusion in his answers about the pants, for example. Was he wearing them or did he sell them... There is an absence of facts about the carrying out of the murder— the scene, events leading up to it— and there are contradictions with earlier statements. All this is compatible with a fabricated memory."

"Now, how would a man like Mr. Brown respond to questioning by police?"

"I found Mr. Brown to be an extremely considerate, moralistic personality. He goes to great pains to be polite— asking me, for example, if I would like one of his cigarettes, then if I would mind if he smoked. His strict moral code makes him exceedingly eager to please those whom he sees as representing authority. He is therefore very suggestible, and I found he would adopt my comments without thinking at all about them, or introducing new ideas of his own."

"Was there evidence of this suggestibility in his confession on the tape?"

"Oh, yes. There is his apologetic attitude: 'I wish I could remember,' 'I wish I could help you more,' 'I have tried and tried.' Also his repetition in many spots of the interviewer's exact phraseology shows an eagerness to help out: 'And this was Geraldton?'; 'It must have been Geraldton.' 'You had the gun?'; 'I had the gun,' and so on."

Cosselli pauses. Then:

"Dr. Pryce, why, in your opinion, would a man like Mr. Brown wait all these years to confess? If he felt so badly when he woke up in the railyard, wouldn't his moralistic character have taken him straight to the police right then?"

"Well, as I have said, his fabricated memory may be a relatively recent thing. Also, though, we must remember that possession of a strong sense of right and wrong does not necessarily make a strong character. And I believe that to trust the police with his doubts and fears would have taken more strength and faith in the system than Mr. Brown had. So instead he pushed the murder away... But as he has grown older his defenses against it appear to have weakened. His nightmares have intensified, grown more frequent. The incident began to destroy him. Only then did his family ties, coupled with his strict moral code, lead him to try and 'make a clean breast of it.' The fact that he felt so relieved after confessing tends to indicate that this is what happened."

"Thank you, Dr. Pryce." Cosselli returns to his seat. The beast *Curiosity* murmurs, gurgles, digesting the new information. Then Foss is on his feet and all sounds in the room die.

"Dr. Pryce, you have testified that the accused has a conscience," the Crown attorney's voice is dry, devoid of colour or tone, "but you have also said that that conscience does not necessarily dictate how he lives, is that correct?"

"Yes, that is what I have said."

"You also surmised that the accused arbitrarily attached his guilt to the murder."

"Yes."

"But if this man's conscience did not guide his activities, is it not every bit as valid to surmise that Mr. Brown attached his guilt where it belonged, that the newspaper story brought back his real memory, that he had indeed pulled the trigger?" The volume of Foss's voice has risen, giving Dr. Pryce's mild response the potency of counterpoint.

"Anything is possible, of course, but I would venture to say that the nature of the confessions and the glaring lack of information contained therein strongly suggest otherwise. Also, in my view, this man's personality is not the type that would be likely to commit cold-blooded murder."

"But you would agree that your opinions about what was going on in his mind twenty-five years ago can only be informed speculation, that there is no way psychology can divine for certain what caused the man's guilt?"

A tinge of iciness in the doctor's voice betrays his annoyance.

"We are no more in the habit of divining than you are, Mr. Foss."

"A good deal less so, if you ask me," Cosselli murmurs. Foss shoots him a look, then turns back to his prey.

"No, Doctor, I beg your pardon, it was an unfortunate choice of words. You would agree, though, that your opinions about what went on in this man's mind can, of necessity, be only that: opinions?"

"I prefer to call them inferences, based upon extensive studies and observations of the patient's history and behaviour."

"All right. Now, Doctor, you also stated that the accused is an alcoholic, presumably a man who has been drinking for many years. In general what quality of memory do long-time alcoholics carry?"

"Very poor memories."

"Memories that are full of gaps even about events that they remember participating in?"

"Yes."

"Isn't it possible then that it is simply the alcoholism that explains Mr. Brown's lack of recall of details of the murder?"

Dr. Pryce considers the point before replying:

"Often, in situations such as you describe, where what memory there is is real, exact seemingly insignificant details do emerge from the haze when the person is questioned... I did not see any evidence of this kind of detail in the tape transcript."

"Details..." Foss leaves a pause, looks pensive. "Doctor, would you say that the accused is intelligent?"

"Oh, yes," Dr. Pryce looks across at Rodger, "his intelligence is well above average."

Foss still appears to be thinking.

"So he has a conscience, but this conscience is not necessarily his guide before he acts. He also has a large measure of intelligence which he could presumably call into play after he acts," Foss smiles. "Thank you Doctor, that is all."

Cosselli springs to his feet.

169

"Dr. Pryce, you have given us your educated opinion, based upon extensive testing and a lifetime of experience, as to what happened to this man. You have also stated that he is intelligent. Could he fool you, do you think?"

The forensic psychiatrist allows himself a brief smile.

"I don't see how, Mr. Cosselli, because much of the material upon which I have based my conclusions about his memory and what may have happened to him comes from the statements the police extracted from him. And as the police officers themselves have told the court, he was trying very hard to help them..." Dr. Pryce turns to the judge.

"Naturally, all I can give the court is my professional opinion in this matter, and of course it is only an opinion. That is to say, there is always the possibility that other conclusions could also be valid. But I am of the belief that the accused would have neither the knowledge nor the desire to lead me astray."

"Thank you, Doctor," Cosselli tosses the pencil he has been holding onto the table, and addresses the judge. "My Lord, this concludes the case for the defense on the *voir dire*."

"In that case we will break for lunch," says Mr. Justice Harley. "We will hear arguments on the admissibility of the three statements this afternoon."

Rodger eats his lunch in the holding cells under the courthouse. Bertie goes to the hospital cafeteria next door for sandwiches.

"Here you are, lad: salmon salad."

Why are all these guards Scottish? Rodger finds himself wondering. Are there immigration posters glued to pub walls all over the wild Highlands: 'Unique opportunity in the jails of the New World...' attracting shiploads of uniformed Berties, all of them lining the rails, their round ruddy faces looking west...?

"You all right, Brown?"

"What? Yeah, the brain's a little overheated, that's all. I don't think I'll have any lunch, thanks Bertie. I can't eat." Rodger holds a cigarette up for Bertie to light. His hands are shaking.

There has been so much new information, too much: first all that stuff about his conscience and the drinking. His mother should have heard it... But then there was Foss's suggestion that it is all bullshit, that he is playing with them, holding something back...

Well, you are, aren't you? Even from the girl reporter... Would the psychiatrist have reached the same conclusion if he had known how much detail you do remember, near the end, in the bar? He tries to draw on the cigarette. It makes him feel like gagging.

"There is only one thing to do," he tells a baffled Bertie. "The girl's right, I'll have to tell Cosselli all of it, every last little bit. Now, before it is totally too late."

"Right you are, lad," answers the bailiff, "but first you eat this. Ye needs yer protein."

CHAPTER 11

The jury is still absent. Until the *voir dire* is over, and the statements Rodger made to the police are either admitted as evidence or rejected by the judge, the jury must remain sequestered.

"Peter?"

Mr. Justice Harley hasn't come in yet, but Cosselli does not hear Rodger. The defense lawyer is over by the press table, chatting with me. One hand is in his pocket, jingling his change: tinkle, tinkle, jing; tinkle, tinkle, jing. His black eyes move up to the clock on the side wall, back to me, then up to the clock again... He is nervous.

Well, no wonder, who wouldn't be? His job this afternoon is to single-handedly save Rodger's skin, to deliver exactly the right series of sword thrusts and shrewdly calculated parries...

Behind Rodger, people are swarming in, buzzing with anticipation. Are they here to watch a man hang, a modern version of the raucous crowds who used to jostle around the base of the guillotine?

No, I decide. These people are drawn by the same force that makes them read my news stories: by the possibility of experiencing vicariously the blood and guts of life, and by a desire to know the answers, to unlock the riddle.

Rodger glances back into the courtroom, sees his mother come in. She is leaning on Uncle Art's arm. She glares down the room at him.

He smiles at her. Behind her Margaret shepherds Aunt Bea through the crush of people. Well, at least they will hear Cosselli's summation. They will both understand at last.

A man with television hair hurries down the aisle towards the press table: Ken Doll, I call him, here for the last scenes, so that, even though he has missed the critical information given this morning by the psychiatrist and O.P.P. Inspector Richardson, he will deliver the story's punchline into people's livingrooms at six o'clock, before I have even finished editing my copy.

Cosselli leaves the press table to return to his seat.

"Peter?" Rodger leans out of his prisoner's box.

"Wish me luck, Rodg'."

"Yeah, right, good luck to both of us... But Peter?" Cosselli had been about to sit down. He shoots a glance at the judge's door, comes over to the prisoner's dock.

"Peter, I hate to bother you now, when you're about to..." Rodger takes a breath, "but it's just that there is one more little thing you don't know. Nobody does. And... well you should know it before you stand up and make your pitch for me."

"Oh?" Cosselli leans close, his black eyes looking right into Rodger's eyes, probing his blood vessels... But is that amusement in them?

"Yeah... I—"

But again he has left it too late. The judge's door opens.

"All rise!"

Cosselli puts a hand on Rodger's arm.

"It'll have to wait." He grins. "You old shyster, I knew all along you were hiding something."

"But it's important to my case!"

"To your case?" Cosselli looks surprised, chuckles. "You let me worry about your case, sport."

"But—"

Cosselli puts a finger to his lips, then, while the judge and then everyone else sits down, he leans over to whisper: "Whatever it is,

Rodg', it doesn't make a damn bit of difference to your case at this point."

"But then how can you—"

"Watch and you'll see," Cosselli smiles. "Trust me."

"Your Lordship," he begins moments later, "the Crown's case, which has kept Mr. Brown incarcerated for the last six months, is based solely upon three statements made by the accused: a verbal confession in a Vancouver bar, a written statement obtained by R.C.M.P. Constables Kilgore and Flowers half an hour later, and a third statement taken two days later by Ontario Provincial Police Detective Inspector Allan Richardson: three statements about a twenty-five-year-old murder, made by a man who at best must be described as vulnerable. That's all the evidence the police have.

"But there are problems surrounding all three of these statements, and that is why I asked for this *voir dire*." Cosselli is speaking slowly, creating with his voice an intimacy between himself and the judge that excludes everyone else in the room, even Rodger.

"I will begin in the bar. Constables Kilgore and Flowers found a man drinking beer. He allegedly told them he had committed a murder— and I stress the word 'allegedly' because there is no written record of this statement nor of anything else that transpired in that bar. Was there any inducement or threat, conscious or conscious? We cannot know..."

Rodger frowns. Both Cosselli and I have explained this question of legal inducement. If someone threatens, or in any way cons you into saying something, what you say does not count in court... But he had called the police himself.

"...We do know that Mr. Brown— then known only as Mr. Jones— was drinking, that he was red in the face, glassy-eyed, crying. We know that he stumbled on the sidewalk on the way out of the bar. Yet these two erstwhile constables insist under oath that there was no evidence of impairment. Why?" Cosselli pauses.

"My Lord, I suggest that these two men did a slipshod job that day. They did not bother to record any of their conversations with the accused. They did not bother to test his breath for alcohol because they thought he was a crank. Later, however, it apparently dawned upon them that the question of his impairment might destroy the credibility of his statement, that a conviction for murder might rest upon the quality of their handiwork. So Kilgore tells us that the man was upset but he was not impaired. That is why they did not test him. The accused had a glass of beer in front of him. But Kilgore could tell conclusively that he was not in any way impaired.

"Your Lordship, I do not believe we can trust the judgement of this policeman any more than we can trust his shoddy work methods. We have no way of knowing how many beers Mr. Brown had drunk before he uttered his alleged confession in the bar. We do know that the man is an alcoholic. He may have been drinking for days..."

Now that you mention it, he had, thinks Rodger... Had that affected what he said? Rodger realizes he has no idea. He has never thought of this before.

"...Therefore, I submit that the Crown has not satisfied its burden to prove the integrity of the verbal statement in the bar.

"Half an hour after his arrival at the police station," Cosselli continues, "when the first written statement was taken, the accused still had not had a breathalyser test. If he had been drinking, the effects of the alcohol would not have worn off. Further to this, there is the conversation between Mr. Brown— then Mr. Jones— and Constable Flowers prior to the taking of the written statement. I submit that this was a very important conversation.

"My Lord, we have here a man who, according to the eminent forensic psychiatrist Dr. Michael Pryce, possesses a deep regard for his family. Here is a man of rigid conscience who wants desperately to do the right thing, but who is also terribly concerned about the effects on his family, so concerned that on the day he goes to the police he makes a point, in spite of his upset state, of leaving his identification at home. He even changes his name. So concerned is he that he tells Flowers: 'I don't want my family involved,' 'I don't want to hurt them.'

"Constable Flowers reassures him that his family 'probably will not have to be involved.'"

Cosselli has been reading from his notes. Now he looks up at the judge.

"But what if the constable had told the accused that his family probably would have to become involved, as was in fact the case? What if he had said: 'I'm sorry, Mr. Jones, but in the end, your family will have to know.' After all, that is usually the case, isn't it? Or what if he had simply said nothing? Would a man so concerned about this issue that he had taken on an assumed name, a man who was emotionally distraught by all accounts, would such a man have gone on, in the absence of the kind of reassurance Constable Flowers gave him, to sign a written statement?

"Flowers says yes. But this one-and-a-half-year constable makes all kinds of blanket statements— about impairment, about the contents of a whole fifteen-minute conversation about which he has recorded nothing but a three-line precis.

"I say no. Of course Mr. Brown would not have given the statement. His need to do right by his family, strong enough to take him to the police after all these years, was also strong enough for him to make certain that his family would be kept out of the affair. 'I don't want them to know,' 'I don't want to hurt them.' Over and over we hear this. Keeping his family out of it was more important even, to Rodger Brown, than his own fate. If Constable Flowers had told him the truth during their conversation, that his family might well have had to be notified, the accused would certainly have refused to take the matter any further."

Rodger is nodding.

"Therefore, I submit that Flowers' comment must be considered an inducement which, however mild, however unintentional, had a profound effect on this particular accused. And statements given under inducement, however mild, cannot be admitted into evidence." Except for the occasional crest of indignation, Cosselli is keeping his presentation low-key, personal, only waving one hand now and then, the other hand firmly anchored in his pants pocket.

Mr. Justice Harley listens quietly, makes a note now and then, gives no sign of what he is thinking.

Cosselli turns his guns on the Crown's heaviest artillery.

"Inspector Allan Richardson arrived from the Ontario Provincial Police's Criminal Investigation Branch in Toronto two days after the accused's detention by the R.C.M.P. officers. No charge had been laid, and during this time Mr. Brown did not consult a lawyer. Inspector Richardson, a seasoned professional, took one look at these dubious circumstances, foresaw correctly the exigencies of the court, and decided to obtain his own statement from the accused, one he could protect.

"'Mr. Jones,' he told the accused, 'if you have spoken to anybody in authority about this case, I want it clearly understood that I do not want it to influence you in your statement. Do you understand?' 'Oh, yeah,' replied Mr. Brown— who was still calling himself Mr. Jones.

"But did he understand?" Again Cosselli appeals to the judge. "What had happened to him during his forty-two hours in jail, with keepers such as Flowers and Kilgore? Who spoke to him during that time? Was anything further said to him about his family? We do not know. We do know that the reassuring Constable Flowers was right there in the interview room, taking down this second written statement for the inspector.

"We also know, thanks to Dr. Pryce, that this is a man so eager to please authority, so eager to 'do right' that he will tell you whatever he thinks you want to hear. 'He will adopt your comments without thinking at all about them,' the doctor has told us. In view of this, I submit that there can be no guarantee that when Mr. Brown— then Jones— said 'Oh, yeah,' he was thinking about the caution at all, let alone applying it to Flowers' comment about his family two days earlier, or to any other unrecorded conversation that might have taken place during those two days.

"I submit that when he gave this second written statement, Mr. Brown still thought his family 'probably would not become in-volved.' Therefore this statement, too, is rendered invalid by Flowers' inducement." Cosselli pauses, turns a page of his notes, then looks back at the judge.

"Finally, we come to the tape recording and its effect on the validity of the statement Inspector Richardson obtained. Let us take a trip back to the Vancouver jail, let us recreate the scene.

"Richardson arrives. He reads Kilgore's statement in which the accused mentions killing a cab driver. He then cautions the accused carefully and takes a second written statement in which the accused says 'I shot him.' The accused signs the statement under a false name. Richardson does nothing about this then or later. He does not want anything to jeopardize the integrity of this statement. He thinks he may have bagged Boucher's killer. After twenty-five years, he is on the brink of solving his revered father's case.

"But the written statement he is able to obtain from the accused is extremely vague and Allan Richardson is a careful man. He wants to clarify it. So he has the accused withdrawn while a tape recorder is hidden in the room. An hour later, Mr. Brown is brought back to answer more questions.

"Were these questions a continuation of the written statement? Of course they were! The contents alone show that. This tape was an attempt to clarify a vague written statement. I asked the inspector: 'Was the tape a continuation or clarification of the written statement?' 'Yes,' he replied.

"Oh, later, when he began to realize the implications of what he had admitted, he changed his reply— and to give him credit, it is a fine line we are drawing here— but in the context of the initial conversation he said yes, he was 'clearing up some points.' Therefore, by law, the tape must be considered part and parcel of the written statement." Cosselli is now completely wrapped up in the logic of his argument. Flipping through different leatherbound tomes, he cites precedent cases to support it.

"...Now, having established the link between the written statement and the subsequent tape, we must examine the tape itself.

"My Lord, this taped interview is the work of a skilled interrogator with a purpose, a man who knows what he wants to hear. It is the fine art of suggestibility carried on in a carefully constructed atmosphere of friendship. Mr. Brown had been in jail, alone, worried, confused, unshaven even for two whole days. Now suddenly all he has to do is follow Richardson's leads— 'You had the gun?' 'I had the gun.'— and the goodwill would continue: 'How do you feel, Rodger?' 'Is it a load off your mind, Rodger?'... Oh, yes, Inspector Richardson is an experienced police officer. He saw the needs of the man he was dealing with and he filled those needs.

The result? 'I wish I could help you more,' says the man who is about to be charged with murder.

"But, note that in spite of all Richardson's sophisticated skill, in spite of all his persistence, and in spite of the accused's eagerness to co-operate, Mr. Brown could not come up with any memory of details. There was no recall of a single intimate circumstance that would have been known only to the killer.

"The bloody cab was found in Hearst. Did he remember stopping in Hearst for gas? 'I really don't think I did,' Rodger says, 'I wish to God I could remember more.' 'How much money did you get from the wallet, Rodger?' 'Oh, I never got any wallet, I had a few bucks in my pocket...'"

Rodger stops breathing.

"...'Why did you do it, Rodger?' Inspector Richardson asks him. 'I have no idea at all. There was no provocation,' the accused replies, 'I just can't figure it out at all.' 'And you had the gun.' 'Yes, I had the gun.'

"But there are no new facts, no freely given details. Nowhere do we hear the little facts that a real memory, however fragmented it is, will recall.

"So, given the nature of the man's answers and the strength of his conscience, it is reasonable to conclude, according to Dr. Pryce, that the answers Mr. Brown gave came from a memory that had been subconsciously fabricated after the event, to fill the black hole of guilt within him. Everything he told Richardson could have been previously conveyed to him through the news, the police.

"Your Lordship, I submit that we must accept Dr. Pryce's explanation of the accused's personality. Here is a man eager to purge his troubled soul, susceptible to suggestion, and here is a tape in which so many questions are leading. All he has to do is repeat the words. I therefore submit that Mr. Brown's answers on this tape

180

must be considered suspect, and that the circumstances under which the taped statement was elicited render it invalid in a court of law..." Again Cosselli launches into a series of precedent cases in which psychological manipulation by the police while the accused was without legal protection have rendered confessions invalid.

Rodger can't stop thinking about his mother: has she been listening? Does she understand what's being said?

"...Having established then, that the tape formed part of the written statement, and that it is inadmissible as a totally voluntary statement of information, I now submit that the tape renders its other half— the written statement of which it is part and parcel— inadmissible with it."

Rodger nods in admiration: yes, Richardson duped him, and he, fool that he was, had followed him like a willing little lamb to the slaughter...

Cosselli, meanwhile, is leaning forward now, his hands on the table.

"My Lord, this court is trying a man for a twenty-five-year-old murder. The police questioned this same man soon after the murder, back in 1947, when they had physical evidence such as the palm print that could have established his guilt or complicity in the case.

"It is likely that Mr. Brown was in the area— his pants testify to that— and perhaps he was even guilty of some kind of mischief. That would provide one of many possible explanations for the unidentified blood on his pants. Those were rough years... But in spite of the pants and his interview with the police in 1947, they did not even suspect him enough to take his prints. They did not arrest him, they do not even appear to have questioned him more than once.

"Twenty-five years later all the police have are three statements taken from a very confused individual under circumstances that at best must be considered dubious. I ask the court to give the accused the benefit of the law now by throwing out all three of these obviously tainted statements."

Cosselli sits down. He has spoken for over an hour. It is as if his voice has become part of the air. Now, in its absence, the room sounds empty. No one moves. Rodger looks up at the judge expectantly. Mr. Justice Harley finishes making notes.

"Mr. Foss?"

The Crown attorney rises, hooks his fingers into his watchpockets. His gown flares at the elbows. Carefully he lengthens the silence, drawing a clean line between his adversary's performance and his own. His tone of voice, when finally he does begin to speak, is one of reason.

"My Lord, despite all my learned friend's legal conflagrations, the indisputable fact remains that Mr. Brown came of his own accord to police after twenty-five years, and said: 'I shot a man.' Three times he said it.

"Now, the defense has tried to make much of the fact that the accused was sipping beer at the time of his first confession, in the bar. But if two officers of the law, one of whom has fifteen years' experience with the R.C.M.P., testify under oath that he was not impaired at one o'clock in the afternoon, then I believe the court must trust that opinion. Vocal confessions are courtworthy; therefore Brown's confession at the bar should be admitted." But Foss does not linger here.

"Mr. Brown went to the station with the officers of his own free will. He was told he did not have to give a written statement, but still he chose to confess. Why?

"Mr. Cosselli would have us believe that the accused was on the brink of a decision at this time, that he still had not decided whether to speak. The defense is suggesting that some profound change came over Mr. Brown somewhere between the hotel and the police station, that when Constable Flowers made an ambiguous comment about his family probably not becoming involved, Brown seized it as a promise, heaved a sigh of relief, made his decision, and proceeded to bare his soul.

"If this had been the case, if Brown had been trying to decide at this point whether or not to confess, then perhaps he would have reacted to Flowers' comment in the way my learned friend suggests. But this was not the case. There was no decision being made at this point. The accused had called the police himself. He had already told them once about the murder. If he was as concerned about his family as Mr. Cosselli would have us believe, why did he speak so readily in the bar? He did not even mention his family in the bar. Why did he consent to coming to the station?

"He did so, My Lord, because his moralistic character had long since made up his mind to confess to this murder. He came because it was the only way, in the end, that he knew how to do right by his family. The possibility of their involvement, I submit, was very much a latter day, secondary concern. And Constable Flowers' comment, in the course of a casual conversation, neither altered nor affected in any way that decision to confess, or the ensuing statements made by the accused. Brown was from the beginning willing, co-operative, eager to confess."

True, true, all of it is true. And somehow Foss's dispassionate voice makes it seem all the more so. I had been so sure that Cosselli was right, that everything made sense. But now...

"There was no inducement present here, My Lord. The written statement taken by the two R.C.M.P. officers was entirely voluntary and must therefore be admitted into evidence at this trial." Foss pauses, consults his notes, then once again gives the judge his attention.

"Finally, the written statement taken by Ontario Provincial Police Inspector Allan Richardson is a model of correct police procedure. The accused was clearly and properly cautioned twice. He was to ignore any previous influences. Did he understand what this meant? Yes, he replied. The question could not have been more clearly asked, and in spite of all the psychiatric evidence we have heard today, the fact remains that the accused is a responsible, very intelligent adult. He understood the inspector's caution.

"He was also cautioned that his statement would be used as evidence at his trial, but after two days of consideration he still made the statement." Foss stands up straight, a pillar of the community.

"My Lord, Inspector Richardson's statement was taken with all the safeguards humanly possible. It was not tainted in any way by inducement or threat. There was no psychological manipulation, no sophisticated interrogation techniques in evidence during the taking of that written statement. It was a simple, routine statement in which the accused said: 'I shot the driver.'" Foss leaves a pause.

Rodger shifts in his seat.

"The statement ended when it was read back to the accused, and he signed it. The written statement must therefore be considered fully voluntary.

"I must disagree strongly with my learned friend's argument that the subsequent tape-recorded interrogation formed part of the written confession. A full hour had elapsed. My Lord, the inspector had just arrived from Toronto. He sat down, read the file and then simply began his investigation. How else was he supposed to proceed, except by talking to the accused?

"'The inspector would like to ask you a few questions,' says Constable Flowers at the beginning of the tape. And that's all it was: questions, a police investigation. As we have just seen with the written statement, Inspector Richardson is a skilled and careful police officer. He knows when he is taking a statement and when he is not. He issued no cautions before the taped session because he was not taking a statement.

"When asked by the defense whether the tape was a continuation of the written statement, Inspector Richardson replied in the affirmative. 'There were just some points I wanted to clear up,' he said. Clear up for his investigation. I submit, Your Lordship, that when Mr. Cosselli asked the question, the inspector had no understanding of the context in which it was being asked. Later, when both Your Lordship and I asked him the same question, he answered 'No.' The tape was not a continuation of the written statement. It was part of the police investigation, was part of a general sequence of questions, but in no way was it 'part and parcel' of the written statement. It was no different in nature from the interviews done the next day or the next week.

"The questions asked in the tape and the manner in which they were asked are therefore not at all relevant to this *voir dire*. Indeed they have nothing to do with the written statement and should in no way jeopardize it." Foss takes a moment to look down at his notes.

Rodger stares at his back: forget the whole truth and nothing but the truth, that is what the man is saying. Forget all the other conversations, all the stuff that had come before and after the written statement, all the really important digging, questioning, probing. Just because he had said the one sentence 'I shot him,' the rest doesn't matter.

"My Lord, I believe this court must thank the eminent Dr. Pryce for travelling here today. His testimony regarding the accused's personality was very enlightening. Mr. Brown, he said, is a man of highly moralistic character, a man whose conscience must, at all costs, even after twenty-five years, be appeased. He has been able, through drinking and other means, to still that conscience, but, in the end, the strong, rigid morals that form the bedrock of his personality have brought him to the police, have forced him to say out loud, more than once: 'I killed a man.'

"Dr. Pryce says that he may have fabricated his memory of the murder. That is an interesting opinion, but it is only an opinion. He has also said that Mr. Brown is a highly intelligent man. Therefore I submit that, though all these character traits may, as the defense alleges, have had a bearing on Mr. Brown's attitude during the investigation of this case," Foss waves his hand, brushing them aside, "they have no bearing at all on the integrity of the written statement.

"My Lord, if I may state it again, the statement taken so scrupulously by Inspector Richardson satisfied every conceivable legal qualification of voluntariness and must, in the interests of justice, be admitted as evidence at this trial. The statement taken earlier by an experienced R.C.M.P. officer is also sound. And although the statement taken in the bar was verbal, I would ask the court to recall that its contents are in keeping with those of the other two statements." Foss looks up at the judge.

"Three times this man has confessed to a murder, My Lord. Three times he has told the police 'I shot him.' The court must see fit to allow him his confessions."

Rodger's mouth feels like sandpaper. An hour ago, he had been elated, a step away from exoneration, from freedom... Now surely he is a man condemned.

The judge makes a final note, then surveys the courtroom.

"This court will adjourn until ten o'clock tomorrow morning, at which time I will rule on the admissibility of the three statements."

Rodger is waiting for me in the lawyer's room at the jail. He gazes out the window at the grey November dusk. Somewhere outside, down in the town— maybe in the same hotel where his aunt and uncle and his mother are staying— the judge is reading his notes, smoking a pipe probably, and making up his mind. Will he accept the statements, or reject them?

If he declares all three of Rodger's statements valid, then Cosselli will probably go after Kilgore, shrivel his credibility in front of the jury. But there will still be Richardson's statement, protected by all those fancy cautions. Cosselli will counter with Dr. Pryce. But given a psychiatrist's opinion against three separate confessions, one taken by a perfect policeman, there is little doubt what the jury will decide: 'The defendant is guilty, My Lord...'

Rodger shudders.

...But will the judge allow all three statements? More likely, he will accept only the one Richardson took, when Rodger must have been sober. Then the jury will hear only one of the confessions, and Cosselli will use Dr. Pryce to raise doubts about it...

...Or the judge might throw out all the confessions. If he does, Foss's case will collapse. Cosselli will win and Rodger will go free.

...And then what? He has come here to find out the truth. Cosselli's version of what happened to him makes a lot of sense. He can believe it... But so does Foss's.

The door opens.

"Brown, you're wanted in the visitors' room," Harry the jailor tells him, "a Mrs. Brown."

I nearly collide with Rodger as he leaves the lawyers' room.

I don't mind. I will go home, have a sherry, put my foot up.

"Maggie's here again," he tells me. "Sorry."

But this time, Rodger's visitor is the other Mrs. Brown: his mother.

I peek into the visitors' room on my way out, see her leaning on Uncle Art's arm. The room's high ceiling makes her look smaller than she is. The dull lighting and scratched plexiglass fade her brown coat and the matching brown, old-lady hat, wash the expression out of her face. Except for the jaw, which still juts out, accusing him, and the old hawk's eyes snapping at him from underneath their hooded lids.

For a moment, Rodger becomes the small boy who has stolen the ice cream. He looks about him for a way to escape. But then he straightens.

Rodger's mother detaches herself from Uncle Art's arm, moves towards him, tottering. I go on my way.

She is too old, he will tell me much later, after the trial is over, far too old to have to see her son behind this plexiglass.

"You shouldn't have come, Mother. It can't be doing you any good."

"It's not. I declare, I never thought I'd see any son of mine in a place like this!" She turns her glare onto the pea-green walls.

But still she is here, come all the way across the country to stand beside him. He blinks, not to show tears.

"Ma." He tries to smile. "How are you feeling?"

"How would you expect me to feel, like dancing on the rooftops?" But underneath the harshness, he catches a glimmer of something other than anger. It brings him the memory of the kitchen back home, how it used to smell of the woodstove and the biscuits she was baking. It had that smell the morning he left for

war, and all those times afterwards when, having answered
Margaret's plea for her to drive him to the hospital in the middle
of the night for morphine, his mother would bring him back to her
house, have him sit by the stove while she got breakfast for his Dad,
Jimmy and Jenny. Now he sees that his mother is here because,
again, she needs him to be all right. The jutting jaw, the hooded
eyes, are due to sagging muscles, loose tissue, age, that's all.

"It's going to be all right, Ma." He smiles again. "Please don't
worry. Mr. Cosselli says there's every chance the judge will throw
out all three statements tomorrow, and then before you know it I'll
be sitting in your apartment having tea with you."

"Tea, you? That'll be the day." She levels a look at him through
the plexiglass. "Rodger, there's just one thing I want to know, one
thing I came here tonight to find out. And that is why."

"Why? Why what, Ma?"

She looks at him, blinks.

"Why I made the statements, you mean?" He nods, "I know,
that is the whole problem: why did I go and tell the police I did it,
if I didn't?"

He pauses, looks for a sign from her. She waits.

"Well, Dr. Pryce, the psychiatrist, explained all that, Mother. I
wish you could have been there this morning. He said it was all a
matter of my conscience. I have this highly developed conscience,
he says. So doing right or wrong matters a whole lot to me. He says
I have a high regard for family and that's true, I do. And because
of all this I probably felt so guilty about the drinking that when I
read about the murder, I thought I must have done it!" He stops,
watches to see if she will accept the idea.

She gives her head one brief shake.

"How any son of mine could stand there and shoot an
innocent—"

"Mother, didn't you hear me? I just told you that the psychiatrist, Dr. Pryce, who knows all about how people think, says I probably never did—"

"But you told them you did."

Rodger heaves a sigh.

"Yes! And that's what I'm trying to explain to you. Apparently, I just told them that so they'd listen to me, so they'd take me seriously, help me get the stuff off my chest."

"You lied to the police so you could get something off your chest."

Oh, sweet Jesus, is there any way on this earth to make her understand? He takes a breath.

"Right. I lied. I told them I had done it when I really had no idea at all whether I had done it or not."

Her head tilts sceptically.

"Look, Mother," he pleads, "this thing has been bothering me for years and years, don't you see that? It's why Margaret left me and—"

"No wonder!"

"— And I wanted to get a trial so the court could sort it all out for me, because I myself could not. And that's the truth. So I told them I shot the guy. And well... maybe, when I said it, maybe I thought I had done it, God knows I felt bad about the whole thing... But really... Well you heard what Mr. Cosselli told the judge. Dr. Pryce says that because I respect authority so much—"

His mother snorts. He struggles to ignore her.

"— I more or less went along with whatever the police inspector suggested to me, and he was one sneaky cop, Mother, let me tell you! Anyway, Dr. Pryce says that I have no real memory of the murder and that I probably made the whole thing up because I felt so guilty and bad about all the drinking I'd been doing."

There is a short silence.

"You told the police you shot a man because you felt guilty about drinking." The way she says it, it sounds silly even to him.

"Damn it, Mother—"

"Don't you swear at me, boy. Just tell me once and for all: did you shoot the man or didn't you?"

He stares at her, opens his mouth, shuts it again. She has not heard a thing he has said. There is only one way to satisfy her and that is to lie again. To tell her he did not shoot the taxi driver, that all this is a ghastly mistake. She might believe him... forgive him. He looks at her tough old face waiting on the other side of the plexiglass and he wants more than anything else in the world to tell her the lie.

But no, having come this far towards the truth, he cannot lie any more.

"I don't know, Mother. Now, I don't think I did... but I still don't know for sure. That's why I came here, don't you see: to find out." He watches her take this in. After a moment, her back straightens, the aged chin comes up.

"Son, if you shot somebody, own up to it like a man. Don't try to tell some cock-and-bull story—"

"Mother, I tell you I don't know!" How can she be so quick to think of him, her own son, as a murderer! "Mother, think about it! Do you really think I am a murderer? You've known me my whole life, for Christ's sake!"

But now her head is shaking.

"You said you shot him, Rodger. Three times you said it. If you didn't know, why would you do that?" She gathers her gloves and purse, pushes herself to her feet. She has tried him and judged him.

191

"Mother!" He does not realize he has come to his feet too, that his hands are balled into fists. She totters away from him, reaches the door.

"Mother, please!"

She does not turn back.

"God damn you, Mother!" A bang, as loud as his pain, then a sharp cracking sound drown his words as inside him something breaks apart. Looking down, he watches in horror as his blood paints a red course along the crack his fist has opened in the plexiglass just above the talk hole: right where his mother's head had been.

CHAPTER 13

It's strange. Rodger knows he is here, sitting on his cot, but he feels so removed. He can feel his body: his legs when he moves them, the throb of his hand under the cast— three broken bones, they said— but it is as if his physical, external self has nothing to do with him, as if he has broken through to some place inside himself where he has never been before. Everything is so clear in this place, every image so cleanly defined, like the veins in a flower petal magnified by a drop of summer dew... or the barbs of a thistle more likely. He stares. There is no judgement in this place, no guilt, no fear, only this crystalline clarity:

You are not my judge, Mother. All my life you have judged me, all my life I have thought I had to measure up to your rules... He sees her now, across the cell where the wall is. Her back in the visitor's chair is stiff...

"When I couldn't measure up to what you wanted me to be, I ran away," he tells her, "I took off to war, to sea... All my life I've been running from you, Mother. Even after I married and left you behind, and then after the murder..."

He had spent the rest of the 1940s at sea, losing himself in the colours, sounds and smells of the world's clamouring seaports, going home only occasionally to see the baby he had left in his mother's care, then when Little Rodger's grey eyes reminded him too much of what he had lost, fleeing back to sea again.

Then the 1949 seamen's strike had stopped Canadian shipping. His train west from the port of Montreal, he recalls suddenly, stopped in Port Arthur, and he walked up the hill to the hotel— the same one in which his family is now staying. The only other occupant of the bar was a short Scotsman with thick grey sideburns and an ancient felt hat slammed down on the back of his head.

"Acch, Billy, bring us ano-o-other!" His rubbery face and red nose reminded Rodger of one of Santa's helpers. "Come to the big city, might as well live 'er up!" he told Rodger.

Rodger smiled.

"Where you from?"

"Geraldton."

"Oh, really?" He struggled to keep his voice casual. "I was there once."

The old geezer nodded.

"Everyone was. Working the mines, were ye? Gold? Bottom fell out of the market, but I still do it. Fer misself, ye know. A little prospectin', pannin' the old mine sites, don't do nobody no harm. Young fellas is all out cuttin' trees now, that's where the money be, but me, I dinna cherish nothin' so much as the look o' that tiny nugget shinin' there in the mud at the bottom of the pan." He shrugged. "And as long as there be enough in it to buy me a wee dram... Thanks, Billy."

"Here," said Rodger as the old man dug into his pockets, "I'm buying... I was in Geraldton just one night, a couple of years ago, in April." He looked into his glass. "There was a murder, out on the highway... You wouldn't happen to know if they caught the guy?"

"Couple a years ago, ye say?" The old man scratched his head under the hat. "Acch, they's all kinds o' doin's up Geraldton way: crazy Finns hangin' theirselves in the bush so's you come on them swingin' up there stiff as a sail in the breeze, then there's the wild-eyed fellas prowlin' round like coyotes..." The old man saw the new glass of whisky coming, raised his hand to take it. "Ah, thank ye son, don't mind if I do."

"This was a taxi driver. They looked all over the country for his murderer— or so I hear." His body on the bar stool was shaking.

"Yeah? Cab driver you say...? Oh yes," the old man nodded. "A Frenchy, I remember. They found him just outside of town in a ditch. Never did get the guy, blamed fool that he was. Shot a man for taxi fare, he did, then left his prints and his pants behind!" He laughed, a high whistle-like wheeze that stopped suddenly. He peered into Rodger's face. "But never you fear, lad, whoever that thievin' murderer was, his own conscience will smite him in the end, you mark my words."

Rodger stared. Was the man some kind of clairvoyant? He seemed to be looking right into him, almost as if he could see, as if he knew... Rodger backed off his bar stool, shaking his head.

"Yep." The old man did not appear to have noticed. "I ain't never seed a man yet can take another's life without payin' for it someway..."

Rodger fled north to the Yukon, to Robert Service country, where men "desperate, strong and resistless, unthrottled by fear and defeat" could make it, where "the strong life never knows harness." And the harsh scrub and rock and rugged mountains that were "the freshness, the freedom, the farness" gave Rodger what he needed for a short while. The explosion of life as spring awakened enveloped him: the new greens dark against sparkling patches of left-over snow, the way red cranberries and purple crocuses grew up overnight; the way a creek could be a silent blanket of blue-white snow one day, then suddenly there would be a crack, loud as a gunshot, and a wall of water would come crashing through the bush, breaking branches, melting the snow so that the next minute the creek would be gurgling happily as if it had always been there; the way two-inch pines were pushing their way up through the mile-long piles of broken rock left by the mining companies' wooden dredges that had once steamed like earthbound ships through these wilderness valleys.

It was not the abandoned dredges or the rotting cabins strewn with trash— records of other men's failures— that took the Yukon's peace away from him, nor even the mosquitoes that seemed as large as grasshoppers. It was the discovery that Robert Service, creator of a world that had sustained Rodger through some of his darkest months, that he had travelled all this way to live in, had been a bank clerk. Service had never known "deaths that just hung by a hair," or "hardships that nobody reckons." These had been figments of his imagination, nothing more. There was no "land to be won by Vikings." All of it had been dreamed up in the little stone bank down at the river's edge in Dawson City. Rodger went home to work the ships that plied the British Columbia coast...

"And all those years it was you, your judgement, I was running from, Mother." He looks at her image, still sitting so stiffly. It is such a relief to really talk to her at last. "But why? Why did it matter so much what you thought?"

A series of family slides comes up on the screen of his mind: there is his father as a young man, his face grinning mischievously under the wavy hair— so like his own; and there is his mother smiling back, but then looking down, away, abashed; her father, Rodger's grandfather, appears wearing his Mormon's black suit... Strange how she had defied him to marry a footloose mechanic. Then, having broken away, had emerged from girlhood to become everything the old man could have wished.

"Do you see Father— another footloose, fancy-free type— in me, Mother? But you loved Father. And he would never commit a murder. So how can you judge me that way?

"How can you believe that I, whom you love too, could be a murderer? How?" He stares at her image, shakes his head.

This is where the real pain is. If she can believe it, no wonder he has.

"...Or is it that you see a part of yourself in me?" he wonders suddenly. "The part that threw caution to the winds that one time, that old Hamish always judged as bad, a piece that should have been cut out in the name of duty, honour, truth..."

The image's eyes are fixed on him, but there is no response.

"Oh Mother," he sighs, "if that is so, it makes you so blind. So blind!" The pain turns back into anger.

"Never once in my whole life have you taken the time to see me, Rodger Pearse Brown, Mother, to know who I really am. If you had, you would know there is a lot more to me than a bunch of chicken-shit police statements... You'd know that in one way I am just like you. I brought myself here, didn't I, looking for truth, honour...?"

And then suddenly he sees that he has been just as blind as she is. Blind to everything, always, except the rules— duty, honour, truth— that he has been running from:

"Honestly, Rodger," Maggie cried just yesterday, "who could possibly know you better than me?"

...Not himself, that's for sure. He has no more idea who he is than his mother does.

"You destroyed us," Maggie said.

She was right. He had left her because he was on the run, had never really thought about what she, or his boys, might know of him, or even about how they might feel on losing him. They would be well rid of him, that's all he had thought...

Well, not quite all.

If he is going to be totally honest now, if he is going to sit here in this new place, and strip away all the layers of guilt and doubt and righteousness, then he has to admit that a part of him— not a big part, but still— was actually glad when he came home from the sea and found her gone.

Glad, yes. He was hurt, also angry, enraged that she had gone off on him and taken his son away from him. He was heartsick, determined to go right away and get her back. As he sat on the sofa in that empty flat, shame that he had left her for so long, had made her so desperate, poured through him...

But behind the pain, shielded by his remorse, a new feeling, white and pure and free as a gull, also stretched its wings. There would be no more rent worries, no more coming home to a homesick Margaret and not knowing what to do, no more day-in-day-out at the shipyard. Full of pain though it was, his heart took flight at the thought. And he felt so guilty.

Always he was so guilty: of having the wrong feelings, of doing the wrong things. Matching his feelings and actions to his mother's judgement, and coming up short.

Coming here was doing more of the same, except that now he was replacing his mother's judgement with that of the court. He shakes his head.

How can he have been so damned naive? He thinks of Foss rocking forward with his fingers in his watchpockets, his gown flaring: a crow picking at the evidence, gobbling only the juicy bits; of Richardson the betrayer; of Cosselli, his defender, who doesn't even need to know the whole truth.

And he sees now that the courtroom is only a kaleidoscope: one of the lawyers makes a pattern of the truth emerge so clearly. Then the other lawyer twists the lens, shifting all the colours and shapes into another clear pattern of the same truth...

"There is no such thing as absolute truth, Mother. There's only justice, creating a kind of order out of all the mess. Laws made by men in the name of justice tell us what 'murder' is, and Foss and Cosselli argue about whether the evidence matches the definition. Mix and match, that's all there is to the Queen's justice. No one tries to understand... any more than you do."

If the judge decides that the statements meet the court's rules and allows the jury to hear them, they'll call him 'Guilty.' If the judge doesn't accept the statements there will be no evidence. He'll be found 'Not Guilty.'

Not 'Innocent,' just not guilty. Because that's as far as justice goes.

"There are no absolutes." He listens to the sound of the words. "No absolutes at all, anywhere in this world, Mother." He leans forward on the cot as if she were really there, facing him.

"Don't you see, Mother: truth, honour, duty, these are only ideals. You can't live them, breathe them, eat them. Real life is too complicated..."

Her image thrusts its chin forward, but behind the harshness in her eyes he sees a glimmer: doubt... love. And suddenly, in the peace of this new place, he can see who she really is: just a young, foolish girl out of the back hills, who upon becoming a mother had felt she knew nothing— except Hamish's lessons— and who had tried so hard, because she loved him. He begins to cry for her.

"Oh, dear Mother, you have missed so much..."

His tears blur his image of her. She begins to fade, except for the hawk's eyes snapping at him, trying one last time to reach him, to stand up for what she believes, what he too must believe.

You said you killed him, Rodger. Why would you say that, if you didn't?

"Oh, Mother..." But she continues to fade. He blinks, trying to bring her back, cannot bear to lose her.

"Mother!"

But she disappears. After fifty-six years her power over him is gone.

He is alone. He sits back against the wall, his knees pulled up to his chin. His injured hand throbs. He holds it up, hugs the blanket around him with his left hand. After a while he wipes his tears away, feels strangely light, as if the inside of him has been washed by a rain, dried on the wind.

All right, so there is to be no final judge for him, on this earth anyway. No one can give him his truth.

"You can, yourself." He looks around. There is no one else here. The voice has come from inside himself.

"Me?" he scoffs, "I tried that with the reporter girl, remember? And as for the trial, how am I supposed to know which me is true? Am I the man Dr. Pryce described, whose only guilt was about drinking too much, the moralistic fellow whose conscience made up the memories?... Or am I the intelligent manipulator Foss described?" Rodger sighs.

Even here, in this new place, it's like looking in the mirror and seeing the face, body and hair of someone you have known all your life, but only by sight. Me, who the hell is that?

The throbbing in his hurt hand is getting worse. He feels nauseated. They have warned him that he might. He lies down on the cot, closes his eyes, sees the little girl in the red dress waving to him on the railway platform in Winnipeg Station, just before he met the French Canadians.

"Use your own self again," urges the voice, "the way you did with the reporter. Look back and see which lawyer's image of you best fits how you felt at the time. Start with this little girl. Remember how good you felt at that moment, how fine...?"

"Yeah... I was so clean, full of purpose after talking to Uncle Art and Aunt Bea. I knew where I was going, that I was going to find Margaret and start all over... And then I met the French Canadians and started drinking..." Rodger sits up suddenly.

"Is that why I felt so guilty when I woke up in Ottawa? It wasn't just the drinking, I'd done that often enough before. Was it the fact that I had fallen off my pedestal? I had gone from a man with a clear, firm, righteous purpose to a stumbling, stinking drunk who did not even know where he was or how he had got there. And if I had sold the pants Uncle Art had given me, wouldn't that have added to the guilt? Wouldn't all that guilt have been enough, after my talk with Uncle Art and the clean, good way I had felt, to make me believe I must be guilty of something truly awful?"

"Maybe," replies the voice, "but what about Foss's view? You were in Geraldton, drinking with the French Canadian, and we know there was a gun. Think now, you were in the bar—"

Funny the tricks a mind on the run will play. Rodger smells flowers, a whole garden full of roses. They smell so sweet. A lazy bumblebee drifts from one to the next. They are wild roses, every shade of pink. Where do they come from?... Aunt Bea's ranch, it must be, behind the kitchen. He will stay here in this memory, sit down on the wooden bench outside her back door, rest in the sun. He is so tired and weak...

No. He pushes the garden away... And now there is the deck of a ship, the sun and the salt wind and the sea rippling blue-green all around him and his heart is so full of gladness. He is whole again, a man who can do a day's work, carry his load, a man who is free! He lifts his face to the wind—

"You're not trying, asshole," says the voice. "There is more in the bar, you know there is. And it's not as if you have any place left to run. Also, you have killed before."

"No!"

"Yes." The other little Italian girl appears, lying in the alley with bits of sand stuck to the blood around her mouth.

"I did not kill her."

"How do you know?"

"No," Rodger shakes his head, hears himself sob. "Anyway I had no choice, don't you see that? I was a gun sergeant doing my job, that's all."

"Against a little girl? What about the feeling, the wild exhilarating excitement as the ground shook from the force of your gun and up the hill the red tiles exploded? Remember the whooping, Rodger."

He squeezes his eyes shut. The nausea is getting worse. He sits up. He may have to throw up.

"Oh, come on, let's not kid ourselves," the voice persists, "you are capable of killing. Also, Foss said you are smart enough to keep some of the memories to yourself. And that's exactly what you did, isn't it? There is more."

Rodger is shivering. The throbbing in his hand has turned to shooting pains.

Wild and wide are my borders,
Stern as death is my sway,
And I wait for the men who will win me
And I will not be won in a—

"Come off it, Rodger."

He stops, tears streaming down his cheeks, dripping off his chin. He is too tired—

But the tears are the beginning of a storm that breaks loose inside him now. Pictures flash by on a high wind that lifts, tears, shatters the only order he has ever known: there are the explosions, the flames, the mangled bodies coming back down the hill, the dust and heat and his thirst, the wild black thrill of igniting the gun against all that... The little girl's large dead eyes, her brother's hatred. Charlie with him, the feel of his arm around Rodger as he held the girl... Another explosion. Charlie gone. Dead.

Thirty years later Rodger huddles on his cot, shaking, until the gale's force spends itself and he can catch his breath, open his eyes. And see.

There beyond the scattering clouds of his dreadful pain and revulsion and guilt, is Charlie. He is standing on the deck of the cruise ship, the sea breeze lifting his dark hair as he pulls on a cigarette, smiles at Rodger; and there he is sprawled beside Rodger on the Sicilian hillside, squirming to get comfortable on the unforgiving ground, talking to Rodger, laughing...

"Charlie loved me," Rodger tells the voice. "You are right, I have been capable of killing. But I have also loved. I loved Charlie... and Maggie— at least I thought I loved her. Who knows, maybe I still do love her in a way— and Little Charlie and Rodg'. And Elsa. Dear God, I do love Elsa... And all these people have loved me back. For some reason, they have loved me too."

"That has to mean something," says the voice.

"Yes."

Outside Rodger's cell, the moon, nearly full, has moved into the barred square of his window. He lies down again. He will rest, just until the pain in his hand subsides a little, then he will go farther with this. He sees his life stretching away in all directions in this new place. He will explore it all.

ᘓ CHAPTER 14 ᗡ

They are all here. Rodger is surprised. He would have thought his mother would have gone home, if he had thought about it at all. But this morning he feels as if he has been far away, as if yesterday were several months ago.

"Okay?" Cosselli nods at Rodger's injured hand. His lawyer's face is colourless, except for the purple rings under his eyes, the face of an actor, drained but tense after the premiere performance, when there is nothing left to do but wait for the reviews, and the stakes are so high...

The big hand of the clock on the wall beside my press table pulls tighter, tighter until finally, with a mighty tick, it snaps Rodger one minute closer to his destiny. I twiddle my pencil.

Beside me, Ken Doll is doodling stick men swinging from the gallows. Jerk. He knows nothing. But he'll have the judge's verdict on television at noon. By the time the *Chronicle-Journal* hits the streets, my story will be stale news.

I'll have to give it a fresh angle, and depth, and colour, the colour of real life... something Ken Doll and his television studio are not equipped to recognize.

Rodger smiles at me. I try to smile back. Objective as I am supposed to be, I can't help feeling nervous.

"All rise!" Then Mr. Justice Harley is sitting on his bench and there is no sign at all on his face of what his decision will be.

"I will deal with the three statements separately," he begins, "bearing in mind that the burden rests at all times with the Crown to satisfy me that the statements were voluntary— that is, free of the fear of prejudice or the hope of advantage." The judge looks down

205

at his notes. Behind Rodger, the silence in the courtroom is absolute.

"The first is a verbal statement. The accused telephoned the police, after which Constables Kilgore and Flowers met him in the bar. They saw him drink from a glass of beer. He showed signs of intoxication but no inquiries were made about how much he had consumed." The judge glances up.

"I would require much more proof to satisfy me that the accused was, at this time, in the possession of all his faculties so that he could appreciate fully the consequences of making the statement. I am not of the opinion, therefore, that this verbal statement satisfies the legal definition of voluntary."

No one moves.

"The written statement taken an hour later is inadmissible for the same reason. In addition, it has been held that even the gentlest inducement will taint a confession.

"Prior to giving this second statement, the accused was told by Constable Flowers that his family would probably not have to be involved in this affair. I am not satisfied that, had the officer said his family would be contacted, the accused would have given the statement. I have therefore come to the conclusion that although the inducement in this case was very slight, it did nevertheless taint this statement." The judge turns a page in his notes. Back in the body of the courtroom a man clears his throat. It sounds like a rockslide. Rodger's shoulders heave as he takes a breath.

"The defense has attacked the statement taken by Inspector Richardson on three grounds. Firstly, that the inducement just mentioned was still in effect. At the beginning of this statement the police officer says, "'If you have spoken to any police officer or anyone in authority, or if any such person has spoken to you in connection with this case, I want it clearly understood that I do not want it to influence you in making any statement. Do you understand what I have just said to you?' The accused replied: 'Oh, yeah.'

"I think it is significant that nothing was said in that caution about an inducement and I think the accused may well have thought that, by his continuing to co-operate with police, his relatives would not be advised. The Crown has therefore not satisfied me that the inducement had been removed.

"Secondly, there is the connection of the written statement to the tape recorded interview." The judge looks at Foss. "The oral statement was a continuation of the written statement. It was taken an hour later by the same officer in the same room. Both must therefore be considered as one and must either go in, or be kept out of the evidence. I see nothing wrong with the techniques used in taking the written statement. However, this is not the case with the oral statement, in which answers were obtained by cross-examination. Dr. Pryce has testified that the accused has the sort of personality that is very susceptible to suggestion..." Inside Rodger, hope flutters it wings.

"...Thirdly, the complete absence of evidence concerning the accused's treatment during the two days he spent in the Vancouver jail after his arrest and prior to the taking of this statement, concerning any conversations he may have had during that time with persons in authority, leaves my mind in some doubt.

"Therefore I have come to the conclusion that the Crown has not satisfied the heavy burden that rests upon it to show that this written statement and the subsequent oral statement were free of prejudice.

"All three statements before this court will therefore not be admitted into evidence.

"Bailiff, bring in the jury."

Ken Doll rushes off to summon a cameraman. The rest of us sit there, absorbing the news, while the judge explains to the jury that there is no more evidence for them to hear, and that since they have heard nothing so far that could establish the accused's guilt, they are directed to bring in a verdict of "Not Guilty."

"Thank you all for the time you have given this court." Then Mr. Justice William Harley is standing, gathering his papers, leaving, and Cosselli is on his feet, pumping Rodger's hand, laughing, while behind them in the courtroom the beast *Curiosity* breaks apart in a hub-bub of talking, gawking, shuffling feet. And now here comes Uncle Art, elbowing his way up the aisle, grinning...

CHAPTER 15

Peter Cosselli is manning the bar in his office lounge when I arrive, notepad in hand. This room, decorated in green and buff, is where he brings clients who are celebrating.

"Rye? Sherry? What can I pour you today, Claire?" Cosselli does not try to hide his excitement. He is the quarterback of the team that has won. He is flying.

"Congratulations, Peter." I glance across at Rodger, who is sitting on the couch sipping a beer. Beside him his mother is nursing a clear drink, gin probably. Her old hawk's eyes examine me with suspicion. "I'll have a beer, please."

Aunt Bea and Uncle Arthur have the other easy chairs so I pull a straight-backed Chippendale away from the wall, raise my beer and smile at Rodger.

"To freedom."

He flashes me his smile. "You're limping."

"Yes. I ran into an obstacle."

He chuckles. "You, too?"

I open my notepad, glance at his mother.

"I know, they're everywhere, aren't they?... So, what are you going to do now that it's over, Rodger?"

"Well, I'll go home, rest awhile. Then maybe I'll get me a nice stationary engineer's job on land, in an apartment building, maybe. Change a few light bulbs, fix a few toilets, nothing too strenuous in my old age."

But there is more. Something more than a broken hand has happened to Rodger. I know him a little by now and my reporter's nose is twitching. But he's not saying, not with his mother right there. So my job is to frame the questions in such a way that he can answer. The old lady is blinking at me, a mother bird willing me to go away.

"Will you be able to forget the murder now?" I have to ask. "As I understand it, you came to court to find out whether you had done it... You really did not know. But now the court has acquitted you on a technicality, on the rules of evidence. So where does that leave you?"

He does not answer right away, and I am aware of a kind of bated breath in the room. Uncle Art shifts his feet and I notice his heavy brogues, the kind with a pattern of holes punched in the leather. Above them, his black-socked ankles look delicate. Rodger's mother's eyes are upon Rodger, but he does not appear to notice. When finally he speaks, the words come out slowly, as if he is working out his thoughts as he goes along. His good hand strokes his cast.

"I have had a lot of time to think in the last six months, and... I have a lot of thinking left to do. That Dr. Pryce helped me a lot. But I know now that the only place I am ever going to find the whole answer is right here." He taps his cast against his chest, then flashes a self-conscious smile around the room...

Back at the office, I type the last paragraph of my wrap-up story:

So finally Rodger Pearse Brown goes free. After twenty-five years of wandering and wondering and six months of waiting in Thunder Bay's jail, his trial here is over. He has won the freedom to take a new trip: through the minefields of his own mind.

The story will follow all my other ones about this strange trial, out on the Canadian Press wire to newspapers across the country, a cornerstone for my career as a journalist, just as I had hoped. I should be elated. But...

"I'm going to miss our evening chats," Rodger told me when I left this afternoon.

"So am I," I replied.

Is that why I am so despondent now? I type "– 30 –," the reporter's code for "the end," and sit staring at it. Then I "x" it out.

I am learning to trust my reporter's instinct. The trial may be over, but the story is not. In spite of all our jailhouse chats, there is still a piece missing. Something more than guilt and vacuous memories brought Rodger Pearse Brown all the way from Vancouver to a Thunder Bay courtroom. Now he is leaving and I still have not got it. That too is why I am downcast.

I catch Allan Richardson reading the evening newspaper in the coffee shop at the Prince Arthur Hotel. He looks more like a business executive in his blue pinstripe suit than a policeman. He glances at his watch, showing his annoyance at being disturbed.

"I won't keep you," I tell him. "I only want to know one thing." My pen and notepad are ready. "You charged Rodger Brown with the Boucher murder, so you must have been sure he did it. What made you so sure? Did you have anything other than his statements to go on?"

"Oh, Brown did the murder all right." Richardson puts up his left hand, counts off the points on his fingers. "One: he knew the body had been found by the grader operator. He knew where it had been thrown and that was never reported in the 1947 newspaper stories. Two: he said the driver was shot inside the cab, he knew exactly where the bullet hole was, and none of that was ever reported. Three: he said there was a French Canadian and that the gun was big. Both check. Four: the trousers place him near the scene at the right time. Five: he said he left the cab in Hearst. That checks. And finally," Richardson puts his hand down and raises his even, handsome eyebrows, "how did he know the murder had never been solved? He knew because he did it. He came to the police of his own accord and told us so." Richardson folds up his newspaper.

"Oh, yes, Rodger Brown is Boucher's killer all right. He's just lucky he got himself a great lawyer."

◖ AFTER ◗

Four years and a flourishing writing career later I can afford the trip that will finish this story— and turn it into a book.

I have exchanged my multi-coloured jeans for the cosy stylishness of wool slacks, my braid for a short shag cut I can wash and shake dry— live and learn, I guess. I fly out of the snow-swept Toronto airport, and three hours later, circle down over the blossoming cherry trees in Vancouver.

Rodger Pearse Brown meets me in the lobby of the small building where he has been living in a one bedroom apartment. He is wearing tight grey jeans, cowboy boots and a short-sleeved shirt. Extending his hand, smiling, he looks a little older, seedier without the benefit of Cosselli's grey suit. But as we go up in the elevator and he chats with an elderly neighbour lady, as he opens his door and waves me in, he is as affable and polite as ever.

"It's not much," he says, indicating a formica-top kitchen table and two chairs, "but I call it home. Or did. Actually, you're lucky you caught me." Boxes, empty, half-full, closed, are everywhere. Through an open door I see a single bed neatly made, and more boxes. "I'm moving up to Prince Rupert next week, got a new job in the pulp mill there."

We sit at the table drinking beer out of cans and talking into my tape recorder. He tells me that when he got home from Thunder Bay after the trial, Elsa was gone.

"I can't blame her, really." He looks at the table top. "I guess the truth is that I loved her a lot more than she did me. Served me right, some would say... I was pretty cut up about it for a while...

"But I was different when I came back, too. After having been cooped up all that time, all I wanted was to be by myself, to smell the flowers and mull things over. So I went out to my sister's place on Bowen Island and just sat... Then later I took different jobs: ship's engineer, firing the boilers. It's not heavy work on the deep sea ships. You just go around squirting oil on the bearings, then wiping it off again, watching the valves and gauges."

"I thought you said you were going to stay on land."

"Yeah, well," he fiddles with his beer can, "that was when I thought Elsa would be here... I did manage an apartment building for a while, but the people were out of my class." He pitches his voice higher, "'Mr. Brown, my toilet's bust.' So then I went to Imperial Oil, but their boiler room is all automatic. I was nothing more than a janitor. So finally, I went back to the sea, working the tug boats, towing barges full of liquid chlorine to the pulp mills. Or whaling..." He smiles at me.

"I've always been an awful s.o.b. for doing something new. Like the army, all those years ago. My mother was right about that one, I could kick my rear end now. I never should have left school to join the army. But I did it because my buddy did and I had never done it before." He tilts his head back, takes a swig of beer. "Or like the whaling. You don't have to ask questions if you've done something. So one day a few years ago I was sitting in the bar with my pals. 'Ever been whaling, Rodger?' one of them asked. 'No,' I said, 'Why would anyone want to go whaling?'

"They happened to mention that there was a job firing steam on a whaling boat. 'Oh?' I said. Then I excused myself to go to the can and headed right out to B.C. Packers and got the job.

"I had these visions, see, of guys out there throwing harpoons. But I found out the whale never had a chance. They'd bomb it and it just rolled over." Sadness touches his tough, handsome, roustabout's face. He takes another swig of beer, shrugs.

"If you don't get your schooling the only way you learn anything is by actually doing it."

Our beers are almost gone. It is time for me to get what I came for.

"What about the murder, Rodger? Do you still think about it?"

"No, not much any more."

"But you never did get your truth in that court."

"No, I didn't, not straight out. I learned a lot, though." He tells me about punching out the plexiglass and the journey he embarked on that night.

"...And a funny thing has happened since then. I had forgotten that when I passed through Winnipeg one time after the murder, in '48 or '49, I left an extra duffel bag I had with a friend of mine who lived there. He returned the bag a few years later, and I stuck it in my parents' basement. I never opened it until a couple of years after the trial, when my mother was selling the house and I had to clear my stuff out. In it I found a work slip for a job at the mine in Kapuskasing around the time of the murder.

"It was April, remember? So I guess I was going to work up there to get the wrinkles out of my belly until the ice went out of Montreal Harbour."

"So did you go to Kap?"

"Well, no, I never did get there, but Hearst is on the way to Kap. So that explains why I was in the neighbourhood."

"And did the slip bring you back any more memory?"

"No..." Rodger looks relaxed in a way I have never seen him before. "I do remember the French Canadians. I sold one of them my suit for ten dollars— I just hated Uncle Art having to know about that— and the guy got into a fight, just a scrap between friends. We tried to protect him, but he got a bloody nose. That's where the blood on the pants came from."

"Ah." This is new... So am I right, he does remember more than he has ever told Cosselli or me?... Or has this memory been fabricated since the trial?

"...And I remember getting into the hotel in Geraldton. We were short of money and there were all sorts of ideas flying around. The French Canadians had bought the gun in Winnipeg. They were going to rob a bank. So now the big guy said, 'Are you coming, Brown?' and I said, 'Sure, I'll go along with you, but I want to have a little snooze first...'" He is looking past me at the early afternoon light coming in through the curtainless window. Dust motes float in the empty room. "It was a community deal, you see. We were all sitting around on the floor and on chairs in the downstairs bar, a jug of wine between us, and we were passing the gun around." He looks straight at me. I do not breathe.

"I held the gun in my hands, Claire, I do know that. I remember the cold feel of the metal against my palm. I even checked to make sure the damned thing was loaded. It was..."

I wait. He sips his beer, goes back to gazing at the sunlight.

"...And then I remember the French Canadian saying, 'We got a cab. Are you wid' us, Brown?' and I said: 'No, I'm not going anywhere while there's a drink left in the bottle.'"

"So did they wait for you?"

He looks at me again.

"That I truly do not know... I do know that that big French Canadian could have killed a man... But I don't know who actually did it. I know I held the gun, and I know it was loaded... but I wasn't exactly *compos mentis*...

"So that's why, when I woke up in Ottawa and read the paper, I thought I had actually been in a bloody murder. I knew I was with those guys, and there was a loaded gun, I knew I had held that gun and that we called a cab... and there was a lot of blood... and the name Geraldton rang a bell...

"And for all those years after, I thought, 'Geez, I wonder...' At 3 a.m. I'd wake up in a cold sweat, figuring 'Geez, maybe I did do it.' Just like that doctor said. Because they never did get anybody for it. And it seemed to work on me more and more— I guess this is what they call conscience... Anyway, finally it got so bad I couldn't sleep. I got a prescription for knock-out stuff and it wouldn't even fizz. Then Elsa threatened to leave and I thought, 'That's it, I've got to get it over with, find out one way or the other.' Calling the cops was the only way to do that."

"But it didn't work. You didn't find out."

"No. Not in the courtroom. In fact, I got hostile to that prosecutor when I heard him say, at one point in the trial, that I must have done it because how else would I have known Boucher was shot. Foss must have read the same newspaper I did."

"So if you still don't know the answer, how come you aren't worrying any more?"

He sighs, puts down his beer can.

"Well, I guess it all comes down to the fact that, in the end you have to put your faith in something or someone, don't you? I know I was in some kind of bloody mess. But I started to learn something about myself during that trial.

"I've done a lot of wrong to people in my life. I've hurt the people I love most, and I have got into a lot of mischief in my time, getting drunk and into fracases and all, but that cab driver was shot and robbed, and I have never stolen from, or intentionally maimed anyone in my life. I do not take what is not rightfully mine. Call it my 'rigid moral code' if you want, but I believe it is something I would never do, drunk or sober.

"So now I figure that if the due process of the law has cleared me, and if a guy like Dr. Pryce, who knows all about the insides of people, agrees that it's not in my nature to commit a murder, then maybe I can believe that myself." He gives me the brilliant, white, guileless smile.

"When I finally got out of that jail, I knelt down and kissed Her Majesty's soil!"

I cannot help smiling back. I pack up the tape recorder.

"So," he says, eyeing my ring finger, "you broke down and married him."

I feel myself blush.

"Yeah, just last year. A newspaper in Ottawa used the stories I wrote about your trial, and offered me a job... and one thing led to another..."

He grins, delighted.

"So my day in court brought you something too! And here I thought you were going to be one of those women's lib types: freedom before love, and all that."

"I am a 'women's lib type'... But I guess, when you think about it, I came to the same conclusion you did: that in the end the only real answers are a matter of faith. If I believe I can get married and have kids and still keep some control over my own life, then maybe I can." I feel the happiness I have found rising up, like a bubble inside me.

"Though we have had our ups and downs, believe me. John got into this habit of asking me where I was going all the time. Every time I'd go out, he'd want to know where, when I'd be back. When the phone rang, he'd want to know who it was."

"He was jealous."

"No, it wasn't jealousy. He just wanted to know. I think he just didn't want there to be any part of my life that he wasn't in on. But it was driving me crazy. I felt like there was this chain of explanations around my neck all the time, dragging me down. I tried to talk to him about it, but everything I said just went in one ear, out the other. 'I do it because I care,' he kept saying. He just wouldn't understand."

"So what did you do?"

"Well, one day— about a month ago— it was his birthday," I chuckle at the memory. "I came home early to make him a double-decker lemon layer cake, all decorated with swirls and rosettes and writing, and it was not easy, let me tell you. I'm not much of a baker, so I was pretty tense. Then, just before dinner, I realized I'd forgotten to buy candles—"

"Uh oh," says Rodger. I nod.

"Yup. He's stretched out on the couch reading the paper when I put on my coat. 'Where are you going?' He tosses out the question, not thinking as usual. And suddenly I am so mad! I mean here I am trying so hard to bake him a beautiful cake, to make him a happy birthday, and he doesn't even care enough to try not to do what he knows bugs me most. I put down my purse.

"'Where am I going?' I yelled, 'where am I going? I'll tell you where I'm going! Back to the kitchen, that's where!' I went to the cupboard, got out the cake. By the time I came back into the living room with it, he had put the paper down. Seeing the cake, he smiled a little.

"'See this cake, this beautiful birthday cake I made?' I came across the room with it. 'Well, it needs candles. See?' And I squashed it right into his face!" The memory of its feel, of his nose disappearing into it, the yellow icing sticking to his eyebrows, the globs of goo sliding down his cheeks, most of all of the way John's eyes had stared, makes me laugh out loud.

Rodger looks bewildered, does not know whether to see the hilarity or not.

"So... what did he do?"

"He just lay there with cake all over him!"

Rodger laughs a little.

"And did he stop asking where you were going after that?"

"I think he's afraid to... I guess you could say it's not exactly your conventional marriage." I finish laughing. "But so far, so good... Actually most of the time it's terrific."

Rodger gazes at me, then slowly smiles.

"Well, you don't look much like June Cleaver." He glances at one of the boxes on the floor by the wall beside him, reaches down, then hands me a pair of beige lady's tooled leather cowboy boots.

"Here, see if these fit you. I bought them for a girlfriend in Mexico a couple of years ago. But the next morning when I woke up she'd taken off on me. She never even put them on once. Nobody has. Here, try them."

"No, no," I shake my head. They are beautiful.

"Why not?" he asks. "What am I going to do with them? I'm moving to Prince Rupert."

So I try them on. The soft leather moulds to the shape of my feet. He smiles.

"Take them: a belated wedding present, from the man who got you to Ottawa."

Back home I pull out my research from the trial, find the Port Arthur *News Chronicle's* articles written in April, 1947, after Boucher's murder outside Geraldton. The first story tells about the finding of his body, and that the head was crushed. Beside this article is another, smaller one:

Provincial police have been furnished with a complete description of the three men believed to have beaten up and robbed a Port Arthur taxi driver of $20 cash and his taxi and then left him lying in a ditch... The three suspects are said to be French Canadians...

A second News Chronicle article a few days later reports on Boucher's post mortem:

While a manhunt centred on the Hearst area was being pressed for the slayer of Raymond Boucher, the twenty-six-year-old taxi driver whose body was found Tuesday morning lying off the side of the Trans-Canada Highway seven miles east of Geraldton, a post mortem conducted yesterday... revealed the youth had been shot once through the head at close range...

So Richardson is wrong. Rodger did have access to information on both the shooting and the location of the body.

Richardson is also right. Rodger Pearse Brown was definitely present among the drunkenness and violence that stained one northern Ontario night. He remembers blood and he did handle a loaded gun and he had killed before.

But Rodger is right, too. Much as we journalists might wish otherwise, there are no final truths to tell. There are only people's own truths. And in the end the only route to these is a matter of faith.

When the French Canadian asked Rodger, twice, 'Are you wid' us, Brown?' Rodger had said: 'No, I want a snooze...' And, 'No, I want a last drink.'

I stop typing, look down at my new boots. Then type the end of my story:

Rodger Pearse Brown alias Jones may have been present at the beating of a taxi driver one night in April, 1947. That's probably why he remembers blood. He may even have heard the gunshot.

But is he the one who pulled the trigger and took another man's life?

This journalist believes the court's verdict:

Not Guilty.

— 30 —